NEW YORK REVIEW BOOKS
CLASSICS

MELVILLE

JEAN GIONO (1895–1970) was born and lived most of his
life in the town of Manosque, Alpes-de-Haute-Provence.
Largely self-educated, he started working as a bank clerk at
the age of sixteen and reported for military service when
World War I broke out. He saw action in several battles,
including Verdun, and was one of only two members of his
company to survive. After the war, he returned to his job and
family in Manosque and became a vocal, lifelong pacifist.
After the success of *Hill*, which won the Prix Brentano, he
left the bank and began to publish prolifically. During World
War II Giono's outspoken pacifism led some to accuse him,
unjustly, of defeatism and of collaboration with the Nazis;
after France's liberation in 1944, he was imprisoned and held
without charges. Despite being blacklisted after his release,
Giono continued writing and achieved renewed success. He
was elected to the Académie Goncourt in 1954.

PAUL EPRILE is a longtime publisher (Between the Lines,
Toronto), as well as a poet and translator. He is currently at
work on the translation of Jean Giono's 1951 novel, *The Open
Road* (forthcoming from NYRB), and lives on the Niagara
Escarpment in Ontario, Canada.

EDMUND WHITE is the author of twenty-five books, including *The Unpunished Vice: A Life of Reading*, which will
be published in the spring of 2018.

MELVILLE

A Novel

JEAN GIONO

Translated from the French by
PAUL EPRILE

Introduction by
EDMUND WHITE

NEW YORK REVIEW BOOKS

New York

THIS IS A NEW YORK REVIEW BOOK
PUBLISHED BY THE NEW YORK REVIEW OF BOOKS
435 Hudson Street, New York, NY 10014
www.nyrb.com

Library of Congress Cataloging-in-Publication Data
Names: Giono, Jean, 1895–1970, author. | White, Edmund, 1940– writer of
  introduction. | Eprile, Paul, translator.
Title: Melville : a novel / by Jean Giono ; introduction by Edmund White ;
  translated by Paul Eprile.
Other titles: Pour saluer Melville. English
Description: New York : New York Review Books, 2017. | Series: New York
  Review Books Classics
Identifiers: LCCN 2017008613 (print) | LCCN 2017008639 (ebook) | ISBN
  9781681371375 (paperback) | ISBN 9781681371382 (epub)
Subjects: LCSH: Melville, Herman, 1819–1891—Fiction. | BISAC: FICTION /
  Biographical. | FICTION / Literary. | FICTION / Psychological.
Classification: LCC PQ2613.I57 P6513 2017 (print) | LCC PQ2613.I57 (ebook) |
  DDC 843/.912—dc23
LC record available at https://lccn.loc.gov/2017008613

ISBN 978-1-68137-137-5
Available as an electronic book; ISBN 978-1-68137-138-2

Printed in the United States of America on acid-free paper.
10 9 8 7 6 5 4 3 2 1

INTRODUCTION

MELVILLE was a turning point for Jean Giono, the great French novelist, as he made a transition between his Pan Cycle (including the recently translated *Hill*), works of an almost folkloric quality that highlighted his native Provençal landscape, and his Hussard Cycle, in which he invested his extraordinary energies into fashioning unforgettable characters. As he said in a later interview, "In the preceding novels, nature was in the foreground, the character in the background... I called 'chronicles' the whole series of novels which put humanity before nature." The most famous of these chronicles is *The Horseman on the Roof*, which in 1995 the French turned into one of their best historical films, starring Juliette Binoche and Olivier Martinez.

Of course literary things are never that simple. The two cycles overlap; for instance, the characters in the early books are already very strong and the Provençal landscape plays a major role in his chronicles as well. In the foreground of *Horseman on the Roof* may be Giono's very Stendhalian young Italian hero, Angelo, but directly behind him is the flourishing landscape of Giono's province, never more lush than as a background for the devastating cholera pandemic of 1832.

It's very fitting that Giono made his transition during the composition of *Melville*. It must be one of the strangest homages from one major author to another. It began as the introduction to his translation of *Moby-Dick* (the first in French). He worked on the translation with a French friend, Lucien Jacques, and an English antiques dealer, Joan Smith (whom he paid), between 1936 and 1939, though he'd been reading it for years before that. He would take it as his "foreign companion" on his hikes and then sit against a tree trunk and read it in the fields when he had a free moment ... imagining the branches in the wind were rolling waves. *Melville* and the translation of *Moby-Dick* were published separately in book form in 1941. Giono's is still the standard translation into French. Smith had provided a word-for-word translation, though she quickly became irritated by Melville's style. Letters reveal that Jacques did most of the work, but he admired Giono's revisions and additions.

Melville is sometimes called a "literary essay," but in fact it is a short, lyrical novel about Herman Melville, his trip to London in the autumn of 1849 to present his novel *White-Jacket* to his publishers, and his chance encounter with an Irish nationalist called Adelina White (she is purely fictitious). Although, at the beginning, the book sounds biographical, it quickly blossoms into a poetic self-portrait. Giono's Melville is a womanizer, well-recognized, successful, a big, burly man who sleeps in the nude and has a hairy chest. He wears secondhand sailor's clothes, which he much prefers to a top hat and cutaway, his London uniform. An angel challenges him to write a big, important book. Melville resists, exhausted in advance by the prospect, but finally, back in America, he throws himself into the massive undertaking of *Moby-Dick*, which he writes for the beguiling Adelina. Unfortunately, she must have died before she could read it; even on his own deathbed Melville is still hoping to hear from her. She has become his angel. According to Giono, Melville is so depressed after Adelina fails to respond to him, he enters a thirty-year period of silence. (In fact, he immediately wrote *Pierre, or the Ambiguities* after *Moby-Dick*, and then another novel, many stories, the novella *Billy Budd*, poems about the sea, and an epic poem about Jerusalem.)

There were some similarities between Melville and Giono. Melville, as a fierce egalitarian, was against the flogging and severe penalties (Billy Budd is executed) so prevalent on the high seas; Giono was a pacifist, ever since witnessing the horrors of World War I, in which he'd served. When he wrote *Melville* he'd just emerged from prison for the crime of pacifism, which the French state condemned as "defeatism." He would be briefly imprisoned later, during World War II, for "collaboration" with the Fascists. Actually, his biggest "collaboration" was the reprinting of an old photo, without his permission, in a collaborationist magazine. The real problem was that in the mid-1930s he'd broken definitively with the Stalinists, a Moscow-directed French Communist writers' union kept Giono from being published in France from right after the war until 1947.

Both Giono and Melville had overbearing mothers. Both were precocious boys. Both had to drop out of school when their fathers died and both, oddly enough, had to go to work in a bank. Giono had written several folkloric novels, which he felt he could manufacture like little buns, just as Melville had written his maritime adventure stories (*Typee, Redburn, Omoo, White-Jacket*), which seemed to him almost formulaic (*Mardi* is an exception). Shortly after the war Giono began his Angelo Cycle and wrote an unrelated book, his enigmatic, granitic *Un roi sans divertissement* (*A King Without Diversion*, to be published soon by New York Review Books). It was certainly a more ambitious novel than anything he'd penned previously.

Giono had also at this point in his life fallen in love with a married woman, Blanche Meyer, with whom he had an affair for the next thirty-five years. She was Blanche, as her literary double was White (Adelina). Giono and Blanche had a voluminous correspondence. Though they both lived in the same Provençal town of Manosque, they had to be extremely careful about seeing each other. Between 1939 and 1969 he wrote her more than a thousand letters and cards; they are now mostly housed at the Beinecke Library at Yale, but many of them are sealed until a future date. Her letters were burned. She went on to write a tell-nothing memoir about him. Somewhat like F. Scott Fitzgerald with Zelda's letters, Giono apparently ascribed many passages from Blanche's letters to Adelina.

Melville, it seems, was quite different from Giono's portrait. He was infatuated with Nathaniel Hawthorne, who was fifteen years older. For nearly two years the authors saw each other often and talked deep into the night. Hawthorne's wife remarked that Melville wanted more from Hawthorne than he could give. Nevertheless, it was an inspiring period for both men, who felt that the conventional novel of the day had become too narrow a form. During that period Hawthorne wrote *The Scarlet Letter* and Melville wrote *Moby-Dick*, which he dedicated to Hawthorne. When Hawthorne wrote Melville a letter praising *Moby-Dick* (which, in the eyes of many critics, may be the greatest American novel ever written), Melville said, "Knowing you persuades me more than the Bible of our immortality."

Melville, far from the expansive, self-confident man Giono portrays, was in fact touchy, taciturn, and shy—and bisexual.

Giono was the one with the big personality, and the character "Melville" is his alter ego. In point of fact, Giono wasn't much interested in the historic Melville. He was interested in the text and the big, manly Whitmanian figures of the New World. Like many Europeans, after the war Giono was fed up with the timidity of much Continental prose—or its erudition. He turned to Faulkner, Dos Passos, Melville, and to Whitman himself.

Translating *Moby-Dick* was no easy task; rendering Melville's thundering, biblical-Shakespearian prose into French was like translating *Macbeth* into Alexandrines: "*La plus petite chose peut avoir une signification*" doesn't really capture the diction of "the veriest trifles capriciously carry meanings," anymore than "*la joie démoniaque des vagues*" renders the "madness and gladness of the demoniac waves." But the translation is certainly faithful and spirited. The two languages remain essentially different—English with its enormous vocabulary, its Celtic fancifulness, its polyglot origins, and French with its limited vocabulary and strict Academy rules.

Lest we forget, Melville was not just typically Anglo-Saxon. He was one of the strangest, most fanciful of visionaries. Hawthorne noted how restlessly his friend wore himself out going back and forth from being a believer to being an atheist; we could say he was a "mystical atheist." The whalers look into the sea:

> But far beneath this wondrous world upon the surface, another and still stranger world met our eyes as we gazed over the side. For, suspended in those watery vaults, floated the forms of the nursing mothers of the whales, and those that by their enormous girth seemed shortly to become mothers. The lake, as I have hinted, was to

a considerable depth exceedingly transparent; and as human infants while suckling will calmly and fixedly gaze away from the breast, as if leading two different lives at the time; and while yet drawing mortal nourishment, be still spiritually feasting upon some unearthly reminiscence;—even so did the young of these whales seem looking towards us, but not at us, as if we were but a bit of Gulf-weed in their new-born sight.

Later, a black whaler named Pip drowns because his mates fail to save him in their haste to harpoon a whale. Or, they save his body, but his oxygen-starved brain has been destroyed:

The sea had jeeringly kept his finite body up, but drowned the infinite of his soul. Not drowned entirely, though. Rather carried down alive to wondrous depths, where strange shapes of the unwarped primal world glided to and fro before his passive eyes; and the miser-merman, Wisdom, revealed his hoarded heaps; and among the joyous, heartless, ever-juvenile eternities, Pip saw the multitudinous, God-omnipresent, coral insects, that out of the firmament of waters heaved the colossal orbs. He saw God's foot upon the treadle of the loom, and spoke it; and therefore his shipmates called him mad. So man's insanity is heaven's sense....

A page later Ishmael is rubbing the knots out of big vats of whale sperm:

Squeeze! squeeze! squeeze! all the morning long; I squeezed that sperm till I myself almost melted into it; I squeezed that sperm till a strange sort of insanity came over me; and I found myself unwittingly squeezing my co-laborers' hands in it, mistaking their hands for the gentle globules. Such an abounding, affectionate, friendly, loving feeling did this avocation beget; that at last I was continually squeezing their hands, and looking up into their eyes sentimentally; as much as to say,—Oh! my dear fellow beings.... Come; let us squeeze hands all round; nay, let us squeeze ourselves into each other; let us squeeze ourselves universally into the very milk and sperm of kindness.

Would that I could keep squeezing that sperm for ever!

If Melville can invoke both the female and the male principles through the guise of whales, Giono's Melville summons up the whole universe, out riding in a carriage and discoursing with Adelina, in the book's most stunning passages, so poetically and resourcefully translated by Paul Eprile, who has studied the French so carefully and, as an outstanding poet in his own right, has found the exact nuanced wording needed:

So now Herman started to talk about the world that lay before them. He rolled up the sky, from one edge to the other, as though it were made out of colored silk. And, for a brief moment, there was no more sky. Then, after an interval of four hoofbeats at a gallop, he rolled the sky open again, but now it had turned into a huge skin, tightly enclosing earth's arteries and veins.

Herman is able to take a bay leaf and make Adelina fully grasp it, until it is transplanted in her heart:

He made the woods come closer. Had she ever seen a wood the way he was making her see it?

"No."

He revolved it for her, turned it upside down, turned it inside out: the eastern edge, the western edge, the mysteries of the north and the south, the moss, the fungus, the scent, the color.

"Had you seen it?"

"No."

"Have you seen it?"

"Yes."

He sent the woods back to where they'd come from. They retreated, shrank, lay down again at the rim of the horizon. Had she really noticed the birches with their horsehide bark?

"No."

He summoned the birches. And the birches came. She felt them, not just right next to her, as if she was in an ordinary field and had leaned against one; she felt them in her heart.

When he invokes the smell of rain, "He sustained everything else, only he lowered its register, as if he were lifting off, ever so slightly, the pressure from the pedal of a big cathedral organ." Giono's Melville has the power to summon all of nature—like Prospero. It's a strange, erotico-mystic-botanical form of courtship. Prospero? No, like God. Giono, who lost his faith at the end of his childhood, does not hesitate to deify himself ("She could plainly feel that he was granting her his own world"). Even though their romance is chaste (in the book), we can feel her body; when she removes her hoops and gathers up the excess silk around her childlike hips, we can see and touch her.

Both Melville and Giono were pantheists, or animists, if that means they intuited a god in every tree and a goddess in every lake. Melville, like Emily Dickinson, was discovered only in the mid-twentieth century; Giono has yet to be fully appreciated in the English-speaking world.

—Edmund White

MELVILLE

My friend Lucien Jacques* and I began our French translation of Herman Melville's *Moby-Dick* on November 16, 1936, and finished on December 10, 1939. But long before I embarked on this project, for at least five or six years, Melville's book was my foreign companion. I took it with me regularly on my hikes across the hills. As soon as I entered those vast, wavelike but motionless solitudes, I'd sit down under a pine and lean against its trunk. All I needed was to pull out this book, which was already flapping in the wind, to sense the manifold life of the seas swell up below and all around me. Countless times I've felt the rigging hiss over my head, the earth heave under my feet like the deck of a whaler, and the trunk of the pine groan and sway against my back like a mast heavy with wind-filled sails.

Lifting my eyes from the page, I've often thought Moby-Dick was breaching right in front of me, beyond the foam of the olive trees, in the boiling waters of the big oaks. But at twilight, when darkness deepens our inner dimensions, this pursuit of mine, into which Melville drew me, became at once more general and more personal. The imagined spout in the middle of the hills could subside, and the illusory waters receding from my dream could leave the hilltops—where I'd been kept afloat—high and dry.

Even during times of peace (and likewise, in the midst of war), there are tremendous struggles one wages alone. This tumult is silence for everyone else. You no longer need earthly oceans and

---

*Lucien Jacques (1891–1961), an accomplished painter and poet, was Giono's first literary champion, a fellow pacifist, and a lifelong friend.

commonplace monsters; you have your own private oceans and your own personal monsters. (To the end of time, unspeakable internal mutilations will turn humanity against the gods. And men never seek divine glory unarmed. No matter what anyone says.)

When I was left alone in the dark, I had a clearer understanding of the soul of that patrician hero who takes command of *Moby-Dick*. He would accompany me on my homeward path. I never had to take more than a few steps to catch up with him and, once the depths of the shadows were black, to become him. I would reach him with what felt like a single, longer stride. Then it was as though I'd entered inside his skin, my body clothed in his like an overcoat. With his heart in place of my own, I would troll my wounds through the wake churned by a huge creature of the depths.

Man always craves some monstrous object. And his life has no meaning unless he devotes himself entirely to its pursuit. Often, he needs no fanfare of any kind. He appears to be tucked away, quietly cultivating his garden; but, inwardly, he cast off long ago on the perilous voyage of his dreams. No one knows he's gone. For that matter, he looks like he's still here. But he's far away; he haunts forbidden seas. That gaze of his—the one you caught a moment ago, the one that plainly couldn't serve any earthly purpose and passed through material things without pausing—he was gazing that way because he'd just clambered down from a crow's nest. He's the kind of man who was born to survey uncommon spaces. Such is the secret of lives whose contours can sometimes appear familiar; often, the secret of our own. Sometimes the rest of us know nothing about it until the very end: the awful whiteness of an inexplicable shipwreck that suddenly garlands the sky with spray and foam. But—and this is true in the majority of cases—all of this takes place over such vast reaches, and with monsters so enormous, that it leaves no trace, no survivors, "and the great shroud of the sea rolls on as it rolled five thousand years ago."

It was quite easy for me to share my passion for *Moby-Dick* with Lucien Jacques. A few evenings spent pulling away on our pipes by the fire while I translated certain passages, clumsily but with enthusiasm, were enough to convince him. From this point onward, the book became our mutual dream, one we soon wanted to share with others. The matter was settled when we realized that Melville himself was handing us the principles that would guide our work. "There are some enterprises," he says, "in which a careful disorderliness is the true method." This statement corresponded so exactly with our own natures and with the substance of his book, that everything seemed to be settled in advance, and there was nothing left to do but let things take their course. As is said many times in *Moby-Dick*, and far more eloquently than you could ever say it yourself: When the whale has been harpooned, you have no choice but to go after it; when it sounds, you have to wait for it; and when it breaches, you have to go after it again. And so it was accomplished.

A Melvillean sentence is simultaneously a torrent, a mountain, a sea, and, I would have said, a whale, if Melville himself hadn't demonstrated, in peremptory fashion, that it's perfectly possible to comprehend the architectonics of the whale. But like the mountain, the torrent, or the sea, one of his sentences rolls, lifts, and falls in complete mystery. It transports you; it drowns you. It reveals the realm of images in the blue-green depths, where the reader moves like a slimy piece of seaweed; or else it encircles you with mirages and echoes off deserted, airless peaks. It presents you with a beauty that resists analysis but strikes with violence.

We persisted in trying to reproduce its depths, its chasms, its abysses and its summits, its rockslides, its forests, its darkened valleys, its precipices, and the heavy mortar compounded from it all.

—J. G.

In 1849, when Melville returned to America after a short stay in England, he had a strange item in his baggage. It was an embalmed head ... but it was his own. He was familiar with the customs of the South Sea Island cannibals, and to keep company with a head severed from its rightful owner wouldn't have surprised or frightened him. This time, however, it was his own head. He had every reason to spend his days and nights savoring it, detached as it was from his heavyset sailor's body and filled with a scented balm sweeter than a May morning at sea, a May morning on the hills, a May morning anywhere at all; in short, filled with an indefinable and everlasting perfume.

In reality, he'd set out for England with the sole aim of consulting his publishers. By now, he'd already written almost all of his books. Well, from his point of view, he had already written them all. He felt rid of them.

He was six feet tall, twenty-six inches across the shoulders. His face was a little long but well fleshed, with prominent cheekbones, as you'd expect of someone who worked in the open air, and that clean curvature toward the mouth. He was neither fat nor thin. Brown hair, with big waves of lighter auburn, covered his head and fell onto his neck. He kept his locks well enough under control using his fingers as a comb, except for a pair of short, unruly, crow-black wings, muscular and stiff as a bird's, that curled back over each temple. Between these curls, and below his unblemished forehead—satin-smooth and rounded like a little girl's tummy—slept his gray-blue eyes, slightly absent, shaded by well-defined arches and long lashes. At times, at his heart's bidding, these eyes would coat themselves in an enamel of pure azure, almost opaque, like the sky when the August sun assaults it with full force. A fine, straight, prominent nose with flaring nostrils, a brown mustache, and barely a hint of pink inner lip peeking through a beard cut almost square an inch below his chin. And there you have him!

A few more particulars: exactly thirty years of age, born in 1819, the same year as Kingsley, Lowell, Ruskin, Whitman, and Queen Victoria. A good year. Ancestors all of Scottish descent. Able to trace his origins back to Sir Richard de Melville, who'd allied himself to Edward I in the thirteenth century. Ah! It appears that his own father, Allan Melville, was a merchant. You don't come all the way down from the thirteenth century without suffering some wear and tear. On top of that, it would have been monotonous to be linked to kings for hundreds and hundreds of years. What's more, Allan was, in a manner of speaking, almost a noble merchant, an importer whose business required him to make voyages to Europe. He might no longer be related to those numbered kings, but he was still connected to some well-heeled barons and some kings of commerce. When he had no connections, he went to war, brandishing his maritime code, his scales, and his manifest.

Now, in 1814, Herman's father—or, shall we say, in order to become Herman's father—Allan took Maria Gansevoort as his wife. Poor, dear Mama! To be able to think about her now, Herman would be forced to flush the sweet balm out of his head. The loveliest month of May could never have borne any sort of perfume for poor Maria. She was cold, thin, materialistic, dry, methodical, angular, and arrogant. This truly unique specimen, a perfect combination of these various emotional and physical elements, clothed in austere, two-bit fustian and fortified with whalebone stays, became Mistress Melville. She made immoderate use of these womanly restraints, which her son would later mention with such innocent humor. God might have intended her to use them to drape voluptuous fabric around her body! But since her— one couldn't really say tender—youth, she'd torn all the love poems out of her Bible and, though already a mother many times over, she still blushed at the sight of the names of Ruth, Esther, Judith . . . those women who, when you came down to it, had put their unmentionable female parts at the service of the glory of the Lord.

She found no rest, except through reading the book of Numbers, where at every turn secondary dictates back up the principal dictates. She loved the part about the building of the Temple, and the details of the treasures assembled to fashion the Ark of the Covenant. She had eight children, like entries in an order book. With each one, she felt ashamed of the bitter, brutal springtime that inflated her hips, and of the nursling hanging from her breast like a comma dangling from a figure eight. Nevertheless, she would return right away, with intense joy, to being the icy-veined mistress of the Melville family's purse strings. Herman, number three of the eight, was given his mother's father's first name. As if he'd been suckled on horseback through chinks in the steel armor of one of Ariosto's female warriors, Herman retained only a stinging and distasteful memory of that extraordinary, tactile delight of childhood: the fondling of his mother's breasts. Oh no, not for him! All the same, he'd always taken the milk when it flowed. Then, as now, a drop on steel was still a drop.

From his infancy, boats and the sea had drawn him powerfully, like all potent drafts that lead to potent disorders. He was barely ten years old when, from New York, he wrote to his father at his shipshape home:

> On this wintery afternoon they took me right out to the end of the jetty that goes the farthest out to sea. There were gigantic waves, higher than mountains. The masts of the ships were lashing the water all around, like whips. And they told me they were lashing the water this way across the whole wide world: at Le Havre, at Liverpool, and right in the port of London.

His childhood was perfectly normal, but his father would say, "He's very late to start talking and he seems to be a bit slow-witted." Yes, true, when it came to numbers. West, his teacher at the Albany Classical School, would later say, "I remember him well. He was my favorite student. He was completely useless at mathematics, but very strong at translation and composition. He loved to dream things up and write them down, even though, by and large, the majority of his fellow students detested this assignment and looked for any way to avoid it, in spite of all the penalties." By the time West says this about him, Herman, having died in 1891, will already have a head full of earth.

But for the moment, it's full of balm, and May is blossoming in his eyes. His memories are kings: the islands crowned by foaming sunshine; the unbroken silence of the waters crowned by atolls; and the monstrous, erratic crowns of typhoons, like the crowns of Shakespeare's monarchs, rolling through collapsing monsoons. The balm, however, came from a simple crown of thorns. They placed it over his head one day. It sank right down to those unruly wings of crow-black hair that cover his temples. When he was taking it off, he scratched his forehead with a thin, red thorn. He looks at himself in the mirror. There's no longer any trace left on his forehead, but if he touches the spot with his finger, it's still sticky and soft, as though he were touching a honey cake.

When his father died, he had to quit school. Maria rubbed her widow's hands together in anticipation. How could she make use of a fifteen-year-old child in the building of a Temple? Well, at that point you could always turn him into a bank employee. So he started at the New York State Bank, where his uncle was a director. But when they brought him out to the end of the New York jetty, nobody told him that the heart of a poetic child holds more lashing masts and more billowing sails than all the ports in the world rolled together.

And now, here he is within these walls—he of all people—freighted with his squadrons. His wake smells of tar, hemp, wet pine, iodine, shellfish, and clam chowder. It's unbearable. He can't stand it. The next year, he's already gone. Supposedly he's lending a hand to his brother. In reality he's reading, he's studying: He's shifting his fleets into open water.

Nothing prevents us from constantly widening our horizons. The scope of what we can see is limited only by the length of our stride and, accordingly, by our own powers. Another year and here he is already on his uncle's farm near Pittsfield, Massachusetts. Without realizing it, he's racing to leeward ahead of a storm that's pursuing him. He's sailing out past the stony Maria. Instinctively, he knows he's more confident in his maneuvers when he's out at sea. But for the moment: a peaceful respite in the countryside. He writes to his mother that he's the only one who's brave enough to get close to the bull. He writes to his brother: "There's nothing left of all the grand designs I had for my life. I'd rather face a really grave danger and finally stop doubting myself."

Springtime has never been so beautiful in the orchards of Pittsfield. The violence of the blossoming amazes the farmers. There's such a heavy mantle on the trees, they're groaning like they've been overloaded with snow. At night, an exceptionally limpid varnish makes even the darkest shapes look green, and the stars seem so close to earth you can almost hear them humming. The wind doesn't just blow, it promenades. An unusual fecundity multiplies the numbers of creatures in nests, in stalls, in cowsheds, in pens, in sties, in hutches. The yearling flocks quiver like an enormous layer of jelly fat over the whole of the United States. Even in the city of New York, they can be heard being born in tremendous numbers, just beyond the suburbs; and the sound of omnibuses, ferryboats, hackney cabs, and drive belts is drowned out by the increasing din of mooing and yapping, the swelling of buds, and the quacking of geese.

Maria writes to the farmer:

A very productive year is in the making. I want you to help him learn what business is all about. Tell Herman I've persuaded my brother to give him fourteen apple trees, the ones behind the cowshed in the big, square orchard. Make it clear: He isn't giving him the land or the trees, he's giving him the fruit. Tell Herman he'll have to pick the apples and sell them. He'll let me know how much he gets for them. For the time being, until the harvest is done, I order you to give him a couple of geese that haven't started laying yet. He'll be just as accountable for these, but with the chicks he'll be free to do as he pleases. He should try to sell them too, to top up his purse. We'll see how much he can get for them. And he also needs to look after fattening a pig.

The farmer is astonished. He replies that, as far as he knows, Master Herman is in New York, safe and sound. He left the farm on March 3 when there was still snow on the ground. It takes a while for Maria to find out, to comprehend, and, finally, to admit that he's aboard the *Highlander*, a merchant ship bound for Liverpool. He'd signed on as a common sailor. Later, recalling this voyage, he'll write *Redburn: His First Voyage, Being the Sailor-Boy Confessions and Reminiscences of the Son of a Gentleman, in the Merchant Service.*

But, like the rest of us, he isn't the product of his own experiences alone. Aside from that, what he's witnessed on this crossing is commonplace for a sea voyage. For a long time now he's been living through much more harrowing passages in his dreams. He'd like reality to live up to them. Above all, he'd like reality to surpass them.

Maria has told herself: "We'll see, we'll see. In spite of it all, he's still my flesh and blood." Yes, and he's really his own flesh and blood as well, or at the very least, it will still be a little while before he produces a Melville flesh and blood wholly apart from Allan and Maria's. When he comes ashore he gives himself a shake, takes a look at the sea, turns his back on it, gives it another look, and finally heads off with his long, easy stride into the countryside.

It's essential that he not go home. Does he take a post as schoolmaster in East Albany merely for the sake of six dollars a week plus lodging? A lodging that consists of a tiny cubicle, but here he reads everything about the sea that he can lay his hands on. It's a brief, cloudy period, three years during which he enlists and dismisses a number of crews, hires captains and then thanks them for their troubles, inspects his hull, has it recaulked, fills his hold, tests the waters, misses opportunities, regrets missing them, lies in wait for more, lets them slip by, sets off listing, comes back to anchor, wears out line and sail lying in port, sleeps on the glassy waters of the harbor, and suffers profoundly to hear, day after useless day, the stem of his prow—the prow he wants bathed in glory—knocking pointlessly against the quay.

When he feels too much of a familiar kind of blood in his veins—his mother's blood—he goes out with some frisky serving girls from the neighborhood to maraud the orchards that surround the school. Or else he stations himself at an open window, with a blowpipe and dried peas, and pelts the top hats as they pass by in the street below. But, how to escape from it all? What's to be done when the spirit of Melville rises up? The one who tears the deck of cards or the petticoat from Herman's grasp, and silently spreads the charts of his life across the table. They're all there, each with its star-shaped wind rose. They show the ocean currents like a monstrous, flowing mane, rolling across boundless reaches where it would be fine to be a man. But he's stuck here, dazed with unhappiness, gazing at these charts on which his course has been plotted out, as though he were staring at Medusa.

Ah! If only Maria knew that her own blood would decide everything in the end! Why, of course, she'd be glad. People don't know her very well. Do you think Herman's state of indecision satisfies her? She's equally capable of getting worked up over abstractions. When she's bent under her oil lamp at night, with her Bible open on the table, the majestic edifice, which rises up from the book like a column of smoke, isn't made of cedar beams and hammered gold alone; in fact, the strongest mortar that holds the consolatory church together is made of angels' wings and faith. And she knows you can build a Temple even out of moving water. The important thing is to build it. And this time it may be Maria's lean, warrior's milk that gives Herman the strength to stride back toward the open sea.

In the middle of December 1840 he arrives at Bedford. He walks the quay and inspects all the whaling ships. They're rubbing their snouts against the trough. Where, now, is the pig he was supposed to be fattening, and what about that make-believe business with the apples, and the bank, and the school, and Betty, and Maria, and the whole of America? He's out at the tip of the peninsula, already farther out to sea than he was at the end of the jetty in New York. The whole of America, like a worn, green rag dangling from the spur of a horseman who's ready to mount, is at his heels.

All right then, kind sir, have you made up your mind? Do you want a draft horse or a racehorse? Do you want to sow seeds for your dreams, or are you in need of an animal that can play polo with your illusions? Is it a nag or a Waler you're looking for? (Yes, kind sir, we use nearly the same word for a horse that plays polo and a boat that goes after whales.) You don't look like the sort of man who works the land, though. If I do say so, it's because of your legs. With legs like yours, it would be a shame to have to saddle a nag just to go at a slow walk from your "home sweet home" to the polo field and back again. To me, you have the look of someone in need of a different kind of excursion. You did well to inquire here. Who suggested our establishment? No one! There now, that's the instinct of a true horseman. We've already fitted out Sir Henry Dana. It's thanks to us he was able to write his famous book, *Two Years Before the Mast*. You're acquainted with him? Oh, I beg your pardon, dear sir, so you're at home here. Any friend of Sir Henry's is a friend of ours. A famous horseman, dear sir! He has sent us lots of clients.

I saw right away that you hadn't come here for an ordinary cob. Where did I see that? In your eyes. What did they show? Ah, sir—they want to play polo. This is a professional observation, pure and simple. Yes, kind sir, they have that sort of otherworldly keenness that can't be mistaken. I'm quite pleased with this way of describing it. I came up with it myself. Yes. And then there are the ones who have a sort of down-to-earth keenness. For instance, when you take a close look at a silver dollar... myself, for instance, I have a keenness that's entirely down-to-earth. I'm very good at giving a dollar a close inspection. I know right away where it comes from, where it is at the moment, and where it's going. But there are others—and you're one of them, don't deny it—who have a keenness in their gaze that's focused outward where absolutely nothing exists. Up in the sky, out at sea, off into space, in a word, out there where I, for my part, see nothing at all. You're one of them. You can swear on your mother's grave that you aren't, but you *are*! You play polo, and, as far as your needs are concerned, I have exactly what's required.

It's the *Acushnet*, a whaler, 359 tons. It's about to sail for Fairhaven, a little whaling port two steps away from here. Just one more word, kind sir. Again, about your eyes. The game is straightforward. It's played by ordinary men. Why am I telling you this? Because your gaze goes ever so slightly beyond the spot where the ball lands, as a rule. But only the tiniest bit, sir, only a few fractions of an inch, I believe. You... why, you look like you can hit the target on a damnably big field. But a whaler is nothing more than a simple ball, sir, it's not a seabird. Or so it seems to me. But you know better than I do. I beg your pardon.

Yes, the horse trader in him has it right. But he's too polite. It isn't by only a few fractions of an inch that Herman looks past the mark, it's by several nautical miles. He'll never be able to fit in with the other players. He plays a game out of proportion with human powers. Even so, for the moment, you can't draw any conclusions from this. Does any boy at his age play a game in moderation?

On the list of the *Acushnet*'s crew, among twenty-two Americans, three Portuguese, and one Englishman, he's inscribed as being a native of New York, twenty-one years of age, residing at Fairhaven (a falsehood invented to shuffle the deck), six feet tall, dark-complexioned, with chestnut hair. It was Valentine Pease, the captain's daughter, who drew up the list. She would have been sitting at the table while her father called out the particulars for each sailor who enlisted. But Valentine was capable, all on her own, of lifting her eyes off the page to look at a boy. In the margin, in front of Herman's name, she wrote down "Squaller." Oh, Miss Valentine! A grumbler? What made you see that in him? He didn't say a thing.

He didn't say a thing, except that he desired sincerely to embark on the *Acushnet* with your father. I assure you, he didn't say another word. Yet it's in front of his name that you mark down "Squaller"? In front of his name alone? When there are three Portuguese and an Englishman, on

top of twenty-two other Americans, it would be quite remarkable if you didn't find anything to say about anyone
else. So what's this all about, marking something down in
front of his name alone? (Another bad turn his own eyes
have done him, I suspect.) You mean he'll be hard to handle?
Yes, of course he will be. Seeing as you examined him more
closely than the others, miss, how could you possibly expect
this young man to play polo like the rest of us, on an ordinary
field? Do you want me to tell you, miss? It wasn't Herman
you were thinking about when you wrote down "Squaller."
There was nothing facing you but two eyes, two eyes looking
right past you. After all, it doesn't concern you when a boy
looks right past you, since you're always sure, in the long run,
to attract his attention back to what you really are: plain
stuff, but rosy-cheeked under your black silk bonnet, with
your golden hair spilling out. No, miss, it was the captain
you had in mind. And that's another matter altogether.

Tell me, miss, has he ever tied you to the mast during a
storm? Has he ever lashed you? Yes, I mean with a whiplash,
on your bare skin? Has he ever stuffed you down in the hold,
bound hand and foot, with only a drop of water to drink?
No? Well, I tell you, he *does* do all these things! And you
know it. And we haven't even mentioned the fact that he's
a rotten commander. He's one of those ... just the way he
says "yes" or "at your service" feels like an insult. Two hundred
pounds of sullen flesh and fifty pounds of corrosive muscle.
Ah, miss, he and Herman will never get along, and you saw
it right away. But you're a true captain's daughter, and even
though the lad's good-looking—with his broad shoulders
and his fierce, shy, poet's eyes—it's him you label as the guilty
one. So much the worse for you, Miss Valentine; he was
worth the taking. And if you'd wanted him, he would have

curled up in your hand like a baby sparrow, just in the nick of time.

When boys like Herman head off to sea, it's because they haven't had a girl next to them who's beautiful enough. What a shame. As you yourself note at the bottom of the list, the *Acushnet* sailed from Fairhaven on January 3, 1841, bound for the Pacific. He went off with the captain. Not with you. So now you see what it costs a young woman to believe that real seamanship has to be tough, in the tradition of the Captain Blighs of this world. And, as for me now, writing the story of Herman's life—you're making me ruin a love scene. You're the first really desirable girl he's come across. I was getting to like you. Now I hold it against you. He's gone off with the captain. At the captain's side, for fifteen months, he plows back and forth across the vast South Seas, never once setting foot on shore. Now here's a proper ration of saltwater for you, my boy. If this is what you were after, here's a really good one. This time, you ought to be satisfied.

He is satisfied. Later on, he'll have his hero say: "I don't see much: nothing but water for a long stretch." And Peleg replies: "Well now, what do you think of your idea of seeing the world? Do you still want to round Cape Horn to see nothing but this? The whole world is right where you stand. There isn't any other."

Yes, the world is nothing but what we make of it. And then, there's what it gives back to us. Friendship and love are feelings without bounds. You can love vast beings, like the mountains or the sea, with the same kind of love you feel for a woman, and the same kind of friendship you feel for a man. And you can be loved by these beings in return. This is our blessing. In the darkest depths of our confusion and disorder, this certainty remains. Even when it's the only certainty we have left, it's enough to make us feel our own grandeur. No one knows this better than Herman. In the fullness of time, drawing on memory (that ocean stretched to limitless horizons), he'll write this sanctuary book, in which humanity can harbor its despair and its desire to persist in spite of the gods.

But the fullness of time has yet to come. He's gliding slowly through the long, sinuous swells of the South Seas. Every now and then he comes a bit closer to being face-to-face with the ocean. He starts out wary and dazzled. What gets to him right away is that monstrous web of tricks and charms. If, at the moment, he were playing a game à la Stevenson, he'd never get to know the high seas as anything but a kind of cordial syrup. But the *Acushnet* isn't a yacht. It's a whaler. And Captain Pease hunts for whales. And while he hunts, he doles out slaps and kicks in the rear. Thousands of times, in a sort of perfect, gigantic, arithmetical progression, he'll blaspheme the name of God with curses that become more and more outrageous and original. He careens around among the sailors like the ball in a game of skittles. Beyond a doubt, he has been created and brought into this world for no other reason than to act as an agent of destruction. He's the sledgehammer, the truncheon, the war club, and the cesspool of the Lord.

Herman grows emaciated. He wastes away. Maybe, after all, nothing has really affected him, except for this sort of roving kick in the rear that radiates out all the time from the captain, like a shaft of sunlight. Something unimportant and not aimed at him in particular. Besides, Herman takes a philosophical view of kicks in the rear: He couldn't care less. Even so, the work wears him down. It beats him up and it toughens his skin. Even though the air here is free, and he can expand his lungs to the full, the skin of his belly shrivels up like an old leather boot. Ah! When, by chance, he has a moment to look himself over from head to foot, he discovers that Mr. Herman of the State Bank has undergone a few small transformations! The first time he was able to wash himself from top to toe, the sponge dropped out of his hand. There's nothing left of him but his formidable shoulders. Right under their blades, you can see his lungs expand and contract. But he could circle his belly with his own two hands, and his thighs are attached to his hips like wooden puppets' thighs—just awkwardly tacked on. It's almost as if you could see the dowels and the rubber bands inside. If he only realized how much his eyes have changed! You can't look straight into them anymore. Or if you do, it's at your own peril. Poor Miss Valentine! You should pray to God that you never run into the "Squaller" again. Because, if he were standing in front of you now, he'd be your lord and master. And you'd be stammering words of a different sort, madly.

For fifteen months, since he went to sea, he's been wrestling with an angel. Like Jacob, he's plunged in darkness, and no dawn comes. Wings—unbearably rigid—beat him, raise him up above the earth, hurl him back down, snatch him up again, and smother him. He hasn't had a moment's respite from the fight. No matter if he's reached his limit; no matter if he's completely worn out; no matter if he sinks like a stone into his berth: He wrestles with the angel. If he's leaping into the whaleboat; if he's riding out an iron-gray tempest; if he's staring into the sickening maw of one of the giant creatures of the abyss: At the very same time, he wrestles with the angel. If he's on watch; if he's trimming the sails; if he's up in the rigging; if he's rendering oil; if he's stoking the fire; if he's standing right inside the charnel house of the Leviathan's entrails: He wrestles with the angel. And when the doldrums weigh like lead over thousands of nautical miles; when all earthly powers are asleep; when even Captain Pease has collapsed with fatigue: He, Herman, wrestles with this dreadful angel who, by doing battle, illuminates the impenetrable mystery of the intercourse between humans and the gods. It's inside of this mystery that his eyes have sight. It's here that they fill with images. It's here that they become tinged with bitterness and tenderness. Stripped to the bone, on the strength of nothing more than the spirit that emanates from his eyes, he could count himself richer than all the emperors and kings of the world put together. He'd already made the decision, but now he'll never bow to worldly laws again.

At last the ship makes the Marquesas and tacks in toward Nuku Hiva. It enters the port and ties up. Without further ado, Herman deserts. He takes off with a shipmate named Richard T. Greene. In the evening, they go down into the ship's storeroom and fill their pockets with sea biscuits. Next, barefoot, in the dark: the gangplank. Then, right away, the blistering beach and the night... a southern night, all green with starlight.

This is not a matter of him running away. Don't imagine for a moment that he was the least bit affected by the captain's kicks in the rear. When you come right down to it, Pease is nothing more than a kind of Protestant Hercules. To be even more precise, Pease isn't out for human flesh. He fuels himself with Quaker oats, which smell like shaving soap. He's only cruel when it comes to money. If he doles out whacks with unconcealed glee, it's because each slap that makes a sailor hop to it more smartly can be translated into dollars and cents. Ten slaps shave almost ten cents' worth of time off the cutting-in of a whale, and thirty whiplashes save almost a dollar. He lashes out the way another man cuts back on his expenses. It's true that, at its logical conclusion, all of this helps stock up Miss Valentine's larder.

But the Marquesans exhibit a cruelty even more directly culinary. They don't lash out. They caress and they fondle, but they kill and they eat when their man is plump and the aroma pleases them. Here, it isn't a question of falling into the clutches of a Captain Pease who'll run you off your feet without letting up so that Miss Valentine can afford the choicest pork chops. Here, you yourself are the pork chop, and the captains of this country will lay you out cold so that their Miss Valentines can sink their teeth straight into your haunches. You are in among the cannibals. But the two rascals hide in the palms and let the *Acushnet* depart. They still have high hopes for the new life that lies ahead.

Blessed are those who walk in the furious beating of the angel's wings.

———

Now he's famous. He's written *Typee*, *Omoo*, *Redburn*, and *Mardi*. *White-Jacket* is about to appear. *Typee*, the tale of his adventures among the cannibals, came out simultaneously in London and New York to huge acclaim. Stevenson declared: "There are but two writers who have touched the South Seas with any genius, both Americans: Melville and Charles Warren Stoddard." This book, by an outlaw, was ironically dedicated to Magistrate Lemuel Shaw of Massachusetts. In August 1847 Herman even goes so far as to marry the daughter of this Lemuel Shaw (Herman never does things by half measures). She's sweet, innocent, clear-eyed, and shyly smiling. On the promenade, she walks with mincing steps as she hurries to keep up with the long, fluid strides of the deserter. She leans on the deserter's arm. For his part, he's preserved that slightly scruffy, ever so seductive look of the rebellious sailor: his head bare and cocked at a rakish angle—just the right pose for a ruffian; his hat in hand, as if he hadn't had the chance yet to put it back on after walking away from a brawl; unharmed, unblemished, barely a hair out of place, his collar comfortably loosened, his head held high, and a fairly handsome knitted waistcoat inside his jacket. Still and all . . . a knitted waistcoat.

All the women who pass to and fro under the towering elms of the promenade find him highly attractive. And the same is true at the roadway in the distance, where ladies draw up their tilburies to tip their parasols in greeting. The couple responds, Mistress Melville with a kind of semi-reverence, and Herman with a casual motion of the hat held at the end of his outstretched arm. Flocks of young women and ladies in pairs come to greet them, pausing to talk and gossip. Surrounding Mistress Melville and Herman there's nothing but the swaying of voluminous skirts. Even Mistress Melville, caught up in this vertiginous swell, rocks back and forth like a domesticated wavelet beside her husband. This is the moment when he, Herman, chooses to stay bolt upright, motionless, stony, and silent, with nothing but a very subtle and very agreeable smile descending mischievously right down into his beard. The company trade compliments, exchange smiles, take their leave, and part. Herman and Mistress Melville go back the way they came; the others return to the end of the promenade, where they wait for him to watch as they spin around and swell their crinolines with that supremely elegant motion known as the "love top." If this move is properly executed, it reveals—and precisely within the bounds of propriety—their delicate feet, their ankles, and the whole embroidered ruffle of their long pantaloons.

Now, here's what he has to say to his wife. (He's just written *White-Jacket*, a bitter, blood-soaked book, a book about desperate combat, a renewed attack against the rule of law, against corporal punishment in the United States Navy.) "Well, it's a shame, my dear, but they aren't going to like me anymore. In everything I've done, I've been going against the interests of plenty of people who will make me pay dearly for it. The commodores guard their privileges jealously. If they could get me into their clutches, I'm sure they'd dress me down in no time. But I only write about what I know, and I know they're plowing up the backs of mates of mine with whiplashes even as I speak."

"They didn't whip you, Herman, did they?"

"They did whip me, my dear, just like the others. The law of the high seas spares no one. No doubt, I'm going to have on my back everything that cries out for democracy without knowing what it means."

"Let's greet Miss Morrow," says Mistress Melville. "She's waving to us over there, from inside her carriage."

"Good day, Miss Gwendoline," says Herman, in a bass voice, while toward the roadway he makes the same little nonchalant gesture with his hat.

The reason he's going to London this time is precisely because of *White-Jacket*. The book is written. He's put all his manly rage into it. Now he wants to have it published with as much fanfare as possible. He wants to move, to outrage, and to heal—even if there's a good chance it will blow up in scandal, even if he himself is likely to perish, utterly, in the uproar of that scandal.

He's an American democrat. He's part of that democracy whose praises Whitman will sing later on, starting with the second poem in his *Leaves of Grass*. Democracy is propelling the whole of the New World into its first explosion of lyricism. "Liberty Poem for Asia, Africa, Europe, and America" is already on Whitman's lips:

> Courage yet! my brother or my sister!
> Keep on! Liberty is to be subserv'd whatever occurs....

France has just been turned upside down by the events of 1848. Americans of all social classes share in the excitement of the French. It's an all-consuming, passionate affair. Everywhere in America, people are discussing it and debating it. Everything else is set aside, everything falls under its spell. Suddenly, at a ball, dancing comes to a standstill. The musicians give up playing; the women fall silent and breathe faster than ever before; the men plant their heels firmly inside their boots. They "discuss it." They discuss it everywhere: in workshops, on city streets, on country roads, out in the fields, in farmhouses, in stagecoaches, in the remotest forests. And all the lone rangers, when the night wind lofts their riding coats behind them, gallop in a dream, immersed in an extraordinary atmosphere of human freedom. On all sides, men rise up—teeth clenched, eyes drunk, hearts pledged— with their scythes, their tongs, their horsewhips. These are impeccable men. A moral stain would kill them more surely than a pistol shot. Freedom is a word that permeates their whole existence, their passions, their work. Its grandeur ignites a fire in their eyes and in their words. Young men give up the company of girls to talk among themselves about democracy and the rights of the individual. They're all in love with France. At the end of the poem he'll entitle "France," Whitman will call her "MY WIFE" ("I will yet sing a song for you, MA FEMME"), because France was the land of liberty.

———

On a Saturday evening in the autumn, Herman arrives in London. He's made some concessions to English propriety. He's wearing a spencer of just the right cut, stirrup pants that tug a little at the backs of his knees, slender boots, and a top hat. Yes, a top hat. How many times did he examine this top hat in his cabin? He kept on taking it out of its box and placing it in his berth. He couldn't imagine he was going to put the thing on, especially with all the familiar sounds of a ship groaning and creaking around him. Oh! More than a hundred times he puffed his cheeks out, as if he were getting ready to send a blast through a blowpipe. Then, in London, he puts it on. And it doesn't look ridiculous at all. Not in the least. Likewise, his long, relaxed stride—a bit of a swagger, which he can't alter; the way he sways his arms and shifts his broad shoulders; the mocking way he holds his head; and the isolation and bitterness of his faraway eyes: All of this goes well. Everything goes so well . . . so very, very well. He arrives at his publishers. As soon as he starts talking, they agree to everything, absolutely everything, no discussion, no reservations of any kind, and they place enormous emphasis on the fact that there really is nothing, Mr. Melville, that we have to say contrary to your wishes. We'll do everything you want. Just give us your manuscript. Hand it over right away. He presents it, they thank him, they express their admiration, they accompany him to the entrance, where they take their leave of him again. So there, it's over. He'd expected some negotiations, but no, it's over, it's done. Over and done with in no time.

He rushes back to his hotel. He has to make an effort to hide a savage guffaw inside his beard. Nevertheless, if he doesn't hurry even faster, he's going to burst into uproarious laughter, right there on the sidewalk. And he knows himself: He'll fling his top hat to the ground and dance all over it, right there in the street. What will the English say? He knows what the English will say. So now he starts to run. Which isn't very good form, all things considered, for a man in a top hat. But, too bad, the important thing is not to be "someone who creates a scandal" in the street, as Maria would say. And it's dusk, so no one sees him running, except when he passes in front of the lamplit storefronts. He races up the stairs of his hotel. Now, at long last, he can dance in jubilation all over his top hat. "Did you call, sir?" the chambermaid comes to ask. "No. Well, yes, wait a moment...perhaps I did. No...after all, no, thank you. *Thank you very much.*" Bewildered, the girl goes out, shuts the door, leans back against the wall, wraps herself in her arms, and laughs, dazzled and captivated at once by the extraordinary charm of this madman.

But with a start, he realizes there isn't really anything to laugh about. It will be two weeks before his ship leaves to return to America. So here he is, held prisoner by London. As long as he was able to picture the city with its publishers' lairs where he ought to be snooping around; as long as there was the possibility of getting involved in discussion, in argument; as long as it should have been leading to something worthwhile, London was still bearable. But now—dark, soulless, noisy—he can't stand it. What kind of a trap has he fallen into? With crystal clarity he understands that if he isn't careful, some crazy misfortune is going to befall him. In the final analysis, it was precisely in the wake of this kind of a Londonesque bout of ennui that a gigantic brawl broke out in Lima. And it was drunken bingeing on this kind of ginger-colored fog that led to the wild masquerade of Shanghai.

The room he's in smells of cigars. The odor of old punch lingers in the tablecloth, and the brown leather wainscoting reeks of men. He feels a dreadful apprehension. He knows that in this place, at any given moment, the irresistible desire to display his masculinity, sailor-style, can grab hold of him. If he has nothing to do but listen to his own thoughts, he'll never be able to stay in step for very long with all these country squires he's meeting on the stairs and in the corridors. The hotel he's landed in is full of rural gentry who've come to London to follow at close quarters the debate in the Commons over Palmerston's policy concerning wheat and potatoes. In Herman's view, anyone who deserves to be called a man has better things to do than to conspire to line his pocketbook.

Down below, in the kitchens, they're shifting copper platters around. This evening, they'll use them to serve up stuffed turkeys, yet again. He'll be able to bear it for one more night, two at the very most. But a fortnight ... no, surely not. He already wants to smoke in the parlor and chat in the smoking room, and he's chuckling inside thinking about what he might be capable of doing in the dining room. He really wants to tell them that when it comes to pounds sterling, he'd just as soon shove them up...well, you know where.

If he does remain here, there's no question about what he's going to do. It's as clear as day: He's going to buy himself a big, white top hat. He's seen some outlandish styles in the shopwindows, tube-shaped headgear fit for the residents of Havana, the kinds of prodigious hats you need only place on your head for everyone you run into to feel offended, even in broad daylight, even in Havana. So all right, here's what he's going to do: He's going to buy himself one of these hats. And put it on. And parade it around here, in the midst of the crowd, in the thick of the pea-soup fog. He'll bring it into the dining room and keep it on his head, like a protest in support of a free America. What the hell! But...no.

No. He looks out the window. For a sensitive man, life is so difficult. But it's full of marvels. A vestige of sunset trails through the muddy sky beyond the rooftops of Holborn, like a weathered feather from a rooster's tail. Down below, in the courtyard, the grooms have hung out three big lanterns. They're currying horses gilded with lamplight and mist. Herman lights a little Manila and goes down to take a look. The stable doors are open. The smell of straw, redolent of high roads and laneways, wafts out. Horse manure is a great poet. Herman plants himself in the middle of the yard, his legs spread wide. The stableboys lift the horses' hoofs and let them drop. The shoes ring out on the paving stones. It's a kind of galloping on the spot.

If anything can cure Herman, it's to be found here and nowhere else. He proffers one of his little cigars. This alone leads to a good ten minutes of conversation about tobacco. The stableboy prefers Dutch cigars. Nevertheless, he eventually gets up from bending over the grooming pail, takes a few puffs, and declares that, all things considered, he could get used to the Manila pretty easily; the main thing is that somebody would have to supply him.

"Right," says Herman, "I want to ask you something. Supposing you had ten days of freedom to do whatever you liked, what would you do?"

"That depends," says the other. "In this 'suppose' of yours, would I be flush or would I be broke?"

"Let's say you had five pounds."

"Five," says the other, "then it's a cinch. I'd take off straightaway for Woodcut."

"What's Woodcut?"

"A village, of course."

"And where is it?"

"Oh, it's out Berkeley way, over there above Bristol."

"And why? What's so unusual about that place in particular?"

"Oh, it's just a little hamlet, like any other."

"So?"

"All right, it's because Jenny's in that place, in particular."

"And who's this Jenny?"

"My sweetheart, of course."

"Very good then, it's settled. Herman here is going to set out for Woodcut. If you have any message I can pass on to Jenny, my good man, don't be shy about it."

"With all due respect, master, I perform that kind of commission myself, but if you do go there, drop by Joshua's place—that dirty swine—at the Sign of the Old Sea-Fish. Tell him to do you a rum the way he does one for Dick. The way he does one for Dick. You tell him that."

Now this is just the kind of adventure Herman likes best. He leaves and heads down toward the port. Now it's a matter of getting some clothes. He's not about to go rambling along the back roads of the Welsh Borders wearing a spencer and fancy boots. Over here, at the back of the dockyards, he should be able to find what he needs. And so he does, in a secondhand shop in Limehouse. As he used to say to Mistress Melville, "When it comes to work clothes, the first ones I try on always fit. It's only fancy, dress-up clothes that I need to have tailored, and they still always feel uncomfortable."

In no time at all, he's found a pair of fine, blue, homespun pants, almost brand-new, just the right length. A bit too big around the waist, but this is easily solved by tightening his belt. He's made a bargain for a striped sweater, not exactly what he was looking for but a good thing to have on hand. It's made from the best-quality Scottish wool, as the Jewish shopkeeper has been telling him, repeatedly. "I know how to look with my own eyes, don't worry, I wasn't born yesterday. Yes, your sweater is made from Scottish wool, but ... do you really want to know? All right then: The sailor who brought it in and sold it to you had just come back from the Indies. Here, take ahold of it and give it a sniff. This particular article has drifted around Benares for a century's worth of Sundays. So don't try to put one over on me."

It is true that, except for his bare head, Herman is still dressed like a gentleman. So you can't blame the old man for trying to swindle him. "I'm in the navy myself, you understand, you old rabbit. I'll give you half a shilling for it." And so he has it for the half shilling. "Don't fret, you'll get your chance to earn a living yet." And then he purchases, this time without hesitation, a splendid old pea coat: roomy, cozy, genuine, worn by rain, wind, and work, the color of night at sea, something worthy of veneration. A true shelter from the storm, a real "sailor's house."

"Say, then, you wouldn't happen to have any shoes? If you do, I'll get changed right away." Yes, the old man has piles of them. "Boots? No. No boots along with these pants, you dear old diddler. Do you want people to take me for a green-horn then, as if I didn't know which end is up? No, I'll tell you now what I need to go along with these pants. I need something supple. Do you know what they're meant for, these pants? Well, right then, you put these on after you've left Sumatra, when you're beating back up the China coasts, when the weather's fine and dry, even if it's on the chilly side, and the wind's full of yellow dust. They're made to be worn with bare feet. So, no question about it: no boots."

His heart was swelling again. Big, ferocious wings were starting to fan him furiously, despite the walls of the narrow shop. The old shopkeeper didn't look very much concerned about the big wings. Yes, he had exactly what was required. And so, since the gentleman had just been speaking of China, it was simply a matter of searching through the pile of shoes to find the very thing he was talking about, with respect to being supple, to being Chinese . . . just a matter of looking through the whole kit and caboodle . . . you'll see what I'm going to dig up for you in here. I know they're in here, I haven't sold them. Ah, here they are! Besides, who else could I have sold them to?

They were Chinese shoes made from elephant hide, as supple as gloves, the toes turned slightly upward in the Ti-betan style; a greenish hide—never polished, never greased—with all of its grain; an item both artistic and practical, something absolutely unusual, yet useful everywhere, a true piece of maritime equipment. You don't negotiate the price of such an article; you want it too much. And they fit, they're exactly the right size for his feet, as long as he wears thick wool socks. So, there we have it. Since he's scored his victory with the sweater, he doesn't bargain anymore. He has much more to do; there are plenty of victories to win. Past victories, fame—all of this has just been capsized and engulfed by the tempestuous beating of the big wings. He's in the process of starting over, with a blank slate. All of the major battles have to be won all over again.

"Yes, that's good, agreed. Quick, show me a place where I can get undressed." Because, he tells himself, if the old man doesn't want to let me into his back room, I'll undress right here, in the middle of the shop, regardless of the glass door. True, it only opens onto a dark alley at the back end of the dockyards, but there are English sailors who pass by, and they're Englishmen first and sailors second. No, no, the back room is entirely at the gentleman's disposal, seeing how much he's just spent. We aren't worried that he'll be after the cashbox. And there really is a child back there, not just someone pretending to be one.

How soft the pants are! How supple the shoes! How good the sweater feels against the fur on his chest! And he knows what, in a minute or two, he's going to experience in the pea coat.

"You wouldn't have a piece of oilskin?"

"Yes, three pence."

"And this strap?"

"All right, four."

"Give it to me. You'll see what I'm going to do with it. Here—hold my spencer."

"The gentleman should sell it to me."

"Ah, no, the gentleman doesn't sell." Herman is chuckling. Ah, no! This makes him think, all of a sudden, about Mistress Melville. What would Betty say if she didn't see her writer-husband come back dressed like a famous author? In an instant, the angel's wings stir up a stifling wind, like smoke from unseasoned wood. "Wait, give me that tea box too. I'll put all the Manilas from my case into it, and I'll keep it in the pocket of the pea coat." He rolls up his spencer, the pants he'd been wearing, and his boots. Using the oilskin, he wraps them into a "sailor-style" package, and slings it over his shoulder with the strap. Forward, march.

He'd put the pea coat on before opening the door, but he waited until he was a bit farther away, in the dark, alone. Then he started to move his shoulders and arms around, and at last he savored the warm dependability of the woolen cloth. The heavy jacket faithfully held its former owner's form and gestures. Now Herman gradually filled it with his own. He knew, when he bought the old sea coat, he was buying a whole person. That's why he didn't bargain over it. You don't bargain over the ghost of a mate: a fellow who sometimes favored his left hand, seeing as he'd worn the armholes evenly on both sides of the jacket; someone who wasn't afraid of catching a sore throat, or else he'd also worn a beard, because the large collar wasn't used to being fastened; something of a fighter, because the right-hand pocket had often been weighed down by the barrel of a pistol; and not very mindful—or, at the very least, more concerned about the figure he cut in the world than about his garments— because he was in the habit of hoisting up his coattails and stuffing his hands into his pants pockets. Which is the right way to present oneself in nautical settings the world over, but it stretches pea coats horribly out of shape. In brief, at the very least it lends them a somewhat peculiar air.

Yes, he must have been one of those finicky rascals. The old sea dog had stuffed camphor into all his gear. Even so,

there's a memory of wind in this woolen cloth. In spite of
the camphor, the wind is in there. This brings salt water to
Herman's eyes. In his mind, he hears rumblings over unbounded reaches. But he's more in tune with the mysteries
of the world than with Palmerston's mundane politics. All
of a sudden, he sees that the zinc shop signs aren't swaying,
that the bits of straw on the pavement aren't flying about,
that the laneway is quiet, that the fog isn't moving. It's his
own, personal wind. "So here you are, back again!" he says.
The battle with the angel has resumed. He'd always suspected
it was only a truce.

He's never breathed a word of it to anyone. But plenty of
times, since he came back from the sea, he's been locked
again in secret tussles with the wing-bearer. While he's been
hunched over his manuscript, alone in his writing room, the
angel has often leapt onto his shoulders from behind and
grabbed hold of him. Grabbed hold of him with the terrible
kind of grip that suddenly twists your neck with a merciless
sort of cruelty. Merciless: oh yes, no question about it! The
cruelty that takes no account of weariness, of wants, of the
right you have to live in peace. A right, after all, that you
possess like everybody else: the right to live peacefully, while
lying a little, ever so innocently, from time to time. Simply
to live, to give up on big ideas and grand resolutions, on
yearnings for sacrifice, for self-denial, for things that are
tough, things that are difficult to accomplish, things to which
you have to drag yourself by the scruff of your own neck,
things that wake you up in the night; to live like everybody
else, with that great, complacent selfishness taught to us by
all the churches and by all the powers that be; to travel the
well-trodden roads, to hold the key to all the unbarred doors
in everybody else's stairwells and corridors, to everybody

else's bedrooms (short of venturing into the bedroom of Henry VIII . . .). To live, with one's wife, one's house, one's garden, one's modest job.

There is no "modest job"! How many times have you reminded me that there is no modest job! A thousand times, a hundred thousand times . . . numberless times. You haven't let me eat one plate of beefsteak and potatoes in peace. My job as a poet—since you say that I am one—my modest job as a poet. To write the books I know how to write. Each one of us does what he knows how to do. To do what's asked of me, what I'm paid for. They ask me for it because I'm good at it, because people enjoy it. They buy it because they know I'm a good worker in this business—I know my trade. I give exactly what they expect me to give.

What? The opposite? You're saying I should give them the opposite of what they expect? What kind of tune are you whistling now? If you went to the shoemaker's, and he handed you a guitar instead of a pair of shoes, what would you say? Yes, I know. You don't need any shoes, or a guitar. All right, stop making that noise with your wings. I know you make music on your own, and you fly. I know you fly through the skies. But men don't fly through the skies. They need to wear shoes, and they're lucky to have somebody to make them.

Are you saying I preach to fill my pockets? Yes, I do preach to fill my pockets. Everybody preaches to fill their pockets. I too have the right. But you just said the word "pockets," and that bothers me. You knew it would, that's why you said it. You know how to get at me, better than anyone else. But you, who pride yourself on so much purity, you, with your wings . . . you know, all the same, what you just said isn't true.

Do you want me to tell you exactly why I preach? I preach so that you'll leave me in peace! I don't deny I should be proud to wrestle with an angel. But I don't give a damn! However glorious it might be to bear the distinction of spending one's whole life in horrible struggles with you, with never a moment's respite, I'm telling you, straight out, that I don't give a damn for that glory and I've had it up to here with that distinction! I have no desire whatsoever to be distinguished. Nothing irritates me more than somebody telling me I'm distinguished because they think it will please me. And I'm never more enraged than when, after you've given me a good thrashing, you end up making me really distinguished, and I can tell it's obvious to other people.

Go to hell! Let me speak! I don't want to be singled out for duty anymore, understand? So there you have it, that's why I preach. The hard things, the bitter cup: They're always meant for me. Don't you see that what I've accomplished already isn't so bad? Five or six books. But maybe you haven't even read them? You have? Well then, you can plainly see that I did what I could. (Would that each of us did as much.) More than one can do? Ah, old friend, that's an easy thing for an angel to say. A man can say it too. But (and this is something you'll never understand, you with your foolish angel's head) when a man says it, he's already done enough; he never intended to do more than he was capable of. Try? Me? Absolutely not, I'm telling you! When your cruelty gets affectionate, that's when I have to be the most guarded. Oh, yes indeed! There's nobody like you for saying you love me, even while you're slapping me back and forth with your wings. I've always been taken in by your tenderness. If not for that, I would have had the upper hand a long time ago. It gives you the advantage.

That's exactly what I'm saying: I do feel that you love me. But, in the end, what's it all about? What is there to strive for? You who are always going on about explanations, I *have* explained myself. Do I have to spell it out for you? I've explained everything I know. Everything. I don't know anything else, and I don't want to know anything else. But you—when all is said and done—do you really want to know? You, who are some kind of prodigy, do you really want me to tell you something that the most intelligent or, really, the most dull-witted of the angels doesn't even know: I have a desire for slippers, like everybody else. But no, I'm not referring to your feet, or to mine either; I know very well that angels have no feet. I know they have nothing but long robes and long wings. Many's the time you've smothered me in all that stuff that smells of vanilla and absinthe. What I mean is, whether you happen to be intelligent or thick-headed, you've never understood that you're on one side of the barricade, and I'm on the other. Don't ask angelic things of a man. I am a man, I want my slippers. I want to live: yes, to eat, drink, sleep. Sleep, do you hear? And afterward, let those who want to explain do the explaining. Me, I've done enough explaining. It's someone else's turn to go without sleep. I want to go out for a walk, I want to go fishing, I want to play a game of patience at my dining-room table. No one man has ever stopped the world from turning.

Ah! You agree with me! So, then what? I've written a few books. They're stories. They're entertaining, that's all. Thank heaven, because I can turn out as many books of that variety as I want to, like hot cakes, effortlessly, with no surprises! What are you saying? That this has nothing to do with heaven? Too bad for heaven. I'll blaspheme if I want to! Make the world turn yourself since, that's right, it's your job. But stop coming around all the time to make a poor devil like me miserable on the pretext that I'm a poet. Do your

promoting on your own. I'm a man like any other. Yes I am!
I *am* a man like any other! Let's get going. Come on, get off
my shoulders! You want to know where I'm going? I'm going
to the bar, that one over there, across the road.

It was a sailors' bar, and hardly anybody was in there at
this hour.

"What'll it be?" says the owner.

"I'd like something to eat." He called out again, "And
some stout."

There were two blokes leaning against the bar. They were
smoking short pipes. The owner came back. He was potbel-
lied, but his fatness started from his shoulders and funneled
down into strong, longish legs. He wore a bib apron. He was
clean-shaven, with a hard, sculpted face. He had a bulldog
jaw, and nostrils with short little hairs, almost red, tightly
curled.

"No chance you've run across any of the lads from the
Royal James?" he asks.

"No, haven't seen them at all."

"You're not off the *Happy Return*, are you?"

"No."

"Looked like you were. Seemed I'd seen you before. All
right, then, what'll you have?"

"Give me what you've got."

"*Natürlich*. Three of them, from the *Royal*, came 'round
after midday to say they'd dine here later. They asked for rice
with crabmeat. I have that, and some codfish soup, if you
want it."

"Go ahead and bring me some. But listen—make sure
there's enough left for them."

"Don't worry. I have enough for ten. They're the kind of
lads you don't want to disappoint, if you take my meaning."

"Well, if that's the case, old boy, give me as much as you'd serve up for two."

From behind, the owner looks even fatter than he does from the front. Don't worry, my boy, if you want to pull the wool over *my* eyes, you'll have to be up bright and early. You can go on till the cows come home before you'll get me to believe in your "boys from the *Royal*." I bet you a week's wages we'll see neither hide nor hair of your boys from the *Royal*. The "boys from the *Royal*" ruse—they use it up and down every coastline in the world, in every tavern that serves meals. I know the ruse—as though I could ever forget it!— it's been used on me a hundred times. But go ahead anyway, my boy. Like you say, don't worry. This evening, I'm busy telling lies to myself, so I'm happy to carry on. I believe you like Scripture. I'm going to partake, on the sly, of the sultan's feast supposedly being prepared for the boys from the *Royal*.

Oh, but the rice is exceptionally good, yes, it really is! Herman, with his mouth full, has given the owner a look, and the bulldog has winked back at him. This is real rice with crabmeat! It's impossible to eat rice like this anywhere outside of the Philippines. The owner must have been a sailor. Herman wolfs down his portion, lifts his finger in the air. The owner stops wiping the glass in his hand. Herman winks and says, "Mindanao." The bulldog says, "Right, Vergara, at the head of the bay," and winks back.

It's superb to pluck the little crabs out of the rice with your fingers, to suck their shells, to lick them all over, lapping up the juices that run from every one of their joints, to open them up with both hands, freely, not giving a damn if the sauce runs into your palms, to suction out all of the green, all of the red, all of the brown they have inside, to run your tongue through the cavity and chew up all of these bits of shell, these bones, this iodine, these flavors of the sea, these juices. Ah, is it ever good! And then, to lick your fingers. Freely.

Once he's finished the crabs, he's completely lost his appetite for the cod soup. It would be colorless and would taste too much of the North Sea. No, he hasn't yet satisfied his appetite for curry, for pepper, for the red, green, and brown heat of crabs, for rice. Nor for the low-lying coastlines, whose sands (which the wind used to whirl about, like ringlets of hair) would continually batter the hillsides, already broken up by the mirrorlike reflections of the rice paddies.

He comes up to the bar and slides the bottom of his empty mug across the zinc.

"So, what now?" asks the proprietor.

"Give me another double serving of your rice. Too bad for the boys from the *Royal*. Oh, and while you're at it," he makes a sign to the other man to lean in closer, and he points to his empty mug, "pour me another stout and spike it with a full shot of gin. It helps build morale."

"You don't look like you're in need of that," says the bulldog.

"You never know."

"You never know," he repeats to himself, as he tucks in to his second portion of rice (it's even better than the first).

He's never been very depressed. At least, he means to say, not depressed like other people. But plenty of times he's been just as unhappy as them, just as hopeless, and wracked by even worse misgivings. The dreariness of the open seas: He felt it like everybody else. He took his hard knocks like the rest of his mates. More than the rest of his mates. His sorrows weren't the kind that faded away at a whiff of vanilla or because dry land had just been sighted. Not in the least.

All the dry land on earth could have come crowding at me in a heap, like a flock of sheep leaping at a man bearing salt, and the sorrow would have stayed put. My sorrow.

I've seen the blackest of depressions pack up and leave, because all of a sudden the wind carried the foul odor of a pigsty, which signals a major landfall three hours ahead of the lookout. But my sorrow stayed steadfast at its post. Don't imagine that anybody could have mastered it by material means. Oh, I know very well, it's entirely my own business. The earth grants me as much as it grants the rest of humanity. The earth grants me *more* than it grants the rest of humanity. But, every time, I think: What's next? I am not a lost child. I don't stick my tongue out at the world's shop-windows. And don't worry, I don't spit at its amusements.

As for good fortune, I've had plenty. I am not a wretched orphan. Fathers and mothers—I have them wherever I turn. I don't ask for charity, I dole it out. I'm a nobleman. If the world is a house, I'm a habitué of the house. I'm acquainted with all its wings, and familiar with its little twists and turns. Homemade gin: acquainted. The same goes for all the shelves of the bar, the wine cellar, the kitchen, the bedrooms, the attic, and the garden. The same for getting soused at home, and for being hungover at home.

I am not a lost child. Do I have places to spend my nights and days? I have them up to my ears—I couldn't possibly have more. I am not a lost child. I'm a lost man, and that's another matter. Wake up in the middle of the night, clamber to the top of the mast and stay there, panting like a seal, watch, wait, heart racing, bang your head against the wall of darkness, wear your eyes out, wear your heart out. What for, after all? Because you're about to reach dry land? I'm glad for you. As for me? Just leave me the hell alone. No thanks. And no, it's not that I'm hopping mad. What's the matter with me? Nothing. Nothing, I tell you. Sometimes, it's happened that I've felt my sorrow subside and then, little by little, disappear and leave me on dry land at last. When dawn breaks with the din of an earthquake, and next, a dead calm falls over millions of square miles of the Pacific; when the ship is rooted fast, like an oak, and a drop of water would sound like the trumpet of the Last Judgment. Three months' worth of wind away from land of any description....

What, you were here the whole time? You came in with me? So you turned up here to pack your big wings inside these four walls? Ah, well then, don't budge, and don't stir up the sawdust. And keep your wings folded; the regulars spit while they're smoking their pipes. All right then, so you saw? I had them spike my stout with some gin. Oh, I know you only too well! The day you'll openly admit that something displeases you will be the day it gets hot at the north pole. You approve? It's just as well you should approve, and just as well you're being an opportunist, because if you didn't approve, it wouldn't make one bit of difference.

You've come in. So far so good. But stick close to my back and leave the regulars the hell alone. They have better things to do than bother themselves with you. For the same reason I do? Maybe. It's possible. I was telling you, before I came in, I'm just an ordinary bloke like everybody else. You didn't want to believe it, and now you're the one who's saying so.

What was I saying, just now, you ask? When? When I was eating my second portion of "rice for two"? You only had to listen more closely. It's personal. Yes, it's personal, there's no need to laugh about it. What's so funny about it being personal? I don't go back over things. I'm not one of those clocks that strike the hour twice. I was talking about the arrogance of the gods, if you really want to know. I was talking about the delirium of weakness and the bitterness of being helpless. About human solitude—that's what I was talking about. You see, if I do have anything to explain (and let me emphasize the "if")…well, then, that's what I'd explain.

He went back into the hotel through the open gate of the service courtyard. In the light of the lanterns the stableboys raised from every side, a stagecoach stood ready to depart. It was the Exeter Mail. He inquired about Woodcut. That carriage would leave the next day, at six in the morning, from a small stable behind Gray's Inn. He should ask for the Bristol Mail, and take it as far as Cricklade. From there, take the Monmouth Mail as far as…. All of their advice was full of high roads, branchings off, and no end of places you left by taking shortcuts.

Back in his lodgings, the logs are burning bright in the fireplace, and he doesn't light the candle. He undresses in this dancing flame-light, which exaggerates the shadows of his movements. He goes to bed. Now, in the room, there's nothing but the gentle moaning of the sap simmering at the ends of the logs. He feels strangely free. It's his own free will that's in charge, and his mind is full of projects. He sleeps in the nude—an old habit from his sailor years. Under the fresh sheets, he's splayed open like a starfish. A slow sea-swell lifts and lowers him. "I should never have put that gin in my stout." But he's tough, and nothing can rob him of his senses, except for himself—the sea-swell of his own heart. No, for sure, he has no desire to go on writing the kinds of insignificant books he knows how to write. A life's work is of no interest unless it's a relentless struggle with the great unknown.

It's up to me to devise my own compasses and my own

rigging. In this game, you always set out either to win it all or to lose everything. On account of the book he's just written, the one they're going to publish, he's going to be taken for a rebel. People like to categorize. He's a rebel because he's a poet. But you can really only classify him under his name. He's no more a writer "of the sea" than others are writers "of the soil." He's Melville, Herman Melville. The world whose images he puts into words, it's the Melvillean world. And anything beyond that, praise be to God!

If there's a consistency in his work, it can only be his distinctive style. His titles are, in reality, nothing but subtitles. The real title of each and every one of his books is *Melville, Melville, Melville,* again *Melville,* always *Melville.* I express myself; I'm incapable of expressing any being other than myself. I'm not obliged to create what other people want me to create. I don't get caught up in the law of supply and demand. I create what I am. What I am is a poet.

If he wanted to, he reflected, he could be just as crafty as other people in the publishing trade. But . . . what a meaningless life. They must die of boredom. While he, by contrast, was forever afflicted, forever uneasy, forever out of breath from racing and chasing, always anxious about what was going to rear up around the next bend in the road. Struck down by frightful bouts of hopelessness, by creations that eluded his grasp and crumbled like mud, he would say to himself, "You're a good-for-nothing, incapable of creating anything of lasting significance." And, at other times, buoyed with enthusiasm, he'd say to himself, "Well, there you go, there will always be the petty hangers-on."

People thought he was rich. In fact, he was poor. People told him he hadn't kept a close enough eye on popular tastes and tried to follow them. He would answer, "I'm famous, and there are some poor souls who read me and say, 'There now, that's a decent sort of fellow.' And they're glad to know that a decent sort of fellow exists. What more do you want?" Yes, but it seems he'd been too careless about looking after his own commercial interests. Indeed, they spoke of his "own commercial interests," when in fact he would lose interest in one of his books as soon as it came out, so as to be able to devote himself entirely to the new one he was about to write. "You have to do some promoting," people would say to him. Ah! He did have some promoting to do, but for something other than his books: "Window displays for God the Father's storefront, that's my life work."

He was seeing clearly. He could say it to himself, there, alone in his bed, while a broad smile moistened his whiskers: "I don't live to keep an eye on my commercial interests. I live to keep an eye on the gods." What's more, he'd be ready to earn his keep, starting tomorrow if necessary, doing no matter what kind of work, even something other than writing. Not a "man of letters" in the least.

On this evening, he felt strangely free, strangely decided. He called out softly, "Are you there?" No, the fire was dying out. The embers were crackling, that was all. "*That one*," he said, "as soon as he wins, he takes off. Well, as soon as he *believes* he's won, because—hold on a minute there, boy!— it hasn't been stated yet that I will write this book."

Truly, he didn't feel he was capable of it, unless he had a real change of heart. He looked at the sailor's clothes he'd just bought, lying over there on the armchair. What's he scheming? he thought. What does he have in store for me? What's he going to turn me into?

———

At six in the morning, the sky above Gray's Inn was clear. Delicate cirrus clouds were spread out like an immense wing, exploding with whiteness, in the soaring rays of a green dawn. Moment by moment, new feathers were unfurling, causing tufts of pink air to boil up underneath. "Oh!" says Herman. "This time it's the great game. You're as beautiful as can be! You've given the old outfit a complete shake-up. I've never seen you so lovely. The only thing is, those ... those are wings for a wedding ceremony. Aren't you afraid they'll be a little awkward for traveling? You won't always be flying over open fields where you can spread them out wide. I also plan to stay in little inns. Oh well, so much the worse for you. I've warned you, you'll stay outside. And I might as well tell you straight out, you're sure to make everybody notice us." The first rays of sunlight were beginning to puff up the whole cloud-quilt with gold.

There was no one around the Bristol Mail except for the coachman and the postilion, who were strapping down a chest and two leather bags between the rear springs. The curtains of the coupé were drawn. Herman climbed onto the top deck. After leaving London on the Eton Road, right away the four horses broke into full gallop. The meadowlands were covered with frost. It was only through thousands of iridescent scintillations, like peacock feathers, that you saw the dense greenery of the grasses. Huge groves of sycamores loomed out from the blueness of the mist; they advanced, rearing massive limbs, shrank away from the road and the coach, and retreated across the fields. The coachman's whip tore shreds of smoke from the trees, and the horses' steam flowed and rolled onto the shoulders of the road. The two lead horses galloped, heads down, straining at the bit, legs rounded as though they were rolling up balls of wool; the two wheel horses, noses in the air, shook their manes and whinnied.

The sun was already up when they encountered the first tilbury on its way to London. They saw it turning into the high road from a dirt track. The driver was a short, dark-haired man, very erect, in a tight-fitting jacket and a hunting scarf—which you could see from thirty yards away—wound three times around his scrawny neck. He was endeavoring to get his horse to break into a gallop, without compromising his own upright bearing or his poise. He passed at full speed alongside the carriage. The postilion slapped his thighs in appreciation. The coachman took the opportunity to pass him the reins and warm his own hands, by banging them together inside his thick mittens; then he took hold of the reins again and promptly let the team know he was back in charge.

It was becoming clear that the countryside had awakened before London. They encountered the first market-bound cart. It was sticking to the middle of the road: a wide, slow vehicle, drawn by three horses in tandem. The postilion grabbed hold of his hunting horn and started demanding room to pass, bawling at the cart with long fanfares. Finally, as they were bearing down on top of the cart at full gallop, he stood up on his seat. Leaning forward, he puffed his cheeks out big enough to make his eyes pop. The farmers leapt down to grab on to the bit of their lead horse, and the whole rig pulled slowly off into the field on the left, at the very moment when the Mail coach passed, without slowing, heeling over to the right. The coachman remained motionless, in his thick, fur-lined mantle, his mittens, and the prodigious layer of red fat that padded his hide. All he did was blow steam out past his whiskers. The postilion bemoaned the insufferable task to which he was obliged to devote his earthly existence; he proclaimed it to the entire world, including Herman, in words made inaudible by the rumbling of the iron wheels.

But then they encountered the rest of the carts. They saw a whole line of them, accompanied by people on foot. So the postilion, hanging on to the guardrails of the top deck, began blasting on his horn as though it was the very ram's horn of rage and despair. The astonishing, out-of-breath death rattle of his bellowings made dense flights of larks rise from the most distant fields. And, as though it had been hit broadside by an insurmountable wave, the Mail, almost touching the near bank, flew by the carts at full gallop, straightened itself out on the open road, and continued to race forward, still swaying on its springs, gradually regaining its equilibrium, while little by little the steam puffing out through the coachman's whiskers stopped.

At Paddington they picked up a bag of mail. The borough was coming to life, stretching itself, making squeaking noises from all its storefronts. On his doorstep, a clothier was beating out his merchandise with a cat-o'-nine-tails. Beyond the town, the land became more rugged. The road narrowed and kept the coach to a trot. Wide-open plowlands darkened the terrain. Long streamers of crows flapped heavily behind the teams of oxen who were carrying on with the work.

The coach drove past some horsemen whose mounts were free of baggage. Some of them were heading into the open sea of the fields. Others were climbing, at a walking pace, up dirt tracks toward hills covered in dark-hued woods, from which a fine mist, like tobacco smoke, was streaming. The air was brisk but golden. From every farm along the way, the coach scared up flocks of geese. They tried to take flight and winnowed the lower limbs of the sycamores, furiously flapping their bent-back wings.

The willows hadn't been pruned yet. They were still lifting their branches like trailing red harp strings. Through the deeper-hued branches, you saw the pallor of the sky. There must have been a melody inside those trees, though you couldn't hear it because the wheels were rumbling, the springs were squealing, and the shoes of the four horses were clattering on the road. But when the coach passed right alongside a long barn where they were threshing barley, at the same time you could clearly hear the whole building whistling, "Alexandra, Please." All of England was whistling "Alexandra, Please."

From each crossroads, lanes led half a mile to village squares shaded by huge, almost leafless beech trees. You could see dogcarts pulled up in the squares, and a few men standing around, hands in their pockets, the butcher's boy in his blue apron, pigs squealing. And, as though fixed motionless on a carousel, the whole scene swerved around all of a piece, in time with the four horses straining on the shaft. After the beeches came long lines of poplars, which also swerved around backward; then low-slung thatched cottages, with little arch-topped windows that looked out from under the furry brims of their black straw hats; next came beech groves, with the snouts of houses appearing here and there among the branches; next a long, white wall, overtopped by crosses and an oak, and a second oak; and behind the two oaks a church began not to rise up but to fall away, its stone cross having been the first thing visible among the twisted branches of the oaks; next its compact belfry with its zinc louvers; next its roof; then its stained-glass rose; next its door, wide enough for cartloads of virtuous offerings; next its four

broad steps—they touched the ground just as the Mail passed
by the cemetery gate.

The village offered its houses up to view. Women, shaking
their aprons to shoo the cats away, were herding geese into
their pens. Behind shop fronts and through windows: There
was the shoemaker tapping his nails, the tailor squatting
like a dwarf on top of his table, the embroiderer bent over
her pattern, the minister's fat charwoman with her cross
dangling on her pillowy bosom.

> O! Alexandra, please,
> Ask your heart if there's not a little
> Something there for me.

At his forge, wide open and full of sparks (as though he
were fanning fiery kernels of wheat with wind from hell):
the blacksmith. The postilion and the coachman saluted
him in unison with a shrill whistle. He, in return, struck
four or five hammer blows on the clear-ringing horn of his
anvil. And now...the bridge over the stream: Grab hold of
the handrail, because—there, you see!—before you know
it, you traverse the hump and get to taste your dinner all
over again. Then back out to the countryside, with the high,
dark furrows of the plowlands swerving away in silence,
surrounding the moving coach. Next, some young women,
in skirts caked with mud, returning home heavy-footed
through some fields of beets. They stop to look at the coach;
their weary arms droop from their narrow shoulders. Finally,
much later, next to a somber field, in a wide-open space with
no abode in sight—nobody, nothing else around—a haggard
little boy, all on his own, warming himself in front of a big
blaze of brushwood.

I've never felt so much regret, thought Herman. He leaned forward and looked at the sky. The big wings were still there, high up above. The pale sun imparted such a pure quality to them. . . . they embodied the very indifference and obstinacy of the gods. I've never felt so much regret, he repeated, for not being the person you think I am. As it does everywhere, man's fate shows itself here. It's man's fate one has to express. But, until now, my neck hasn't been squeezed hard enough.

The worst of it, he mused, quite a while later (by now it was almost noon) . . . the worst of it, on top of that, is that I have absolutely no appetite for having my neck squeezed. Which is natural enough. If I sensed something was going to grab hold of my neck, I'd be kicking and screaming like the devil incarnate. No one really goes willingly to anything but celebrations. Who knows what he—*that* other one, up there—will come up with along those lines!

The coach was traveling at walking pace, through rolling country, toward a pass between two hills. The road was closed in on all sides by beech forests. With the onset of autumn, the whole leafy canopy had collapsed; the gray sky penetrated the reddish-brown wreckage and slid down through the branches.

From inside the coach, someone rapped on the window and then opened it. "Jack," spoke a woman's voice, "pull up for a minute at the Dartmoor turnoff."

"Yes, miss," said the postilion.

"There's no passenger but me, is there, Jack?"

"Yes, miss, there's someone, a gentleman, up here with us."

"I beg your pardon," said the voice. Then, after a moment, "Would you permit me, sir, to say a word to some friends who should be waiting for me at the roadside?"

"By all means, madam," said Herman.

"Thank you." And she closed the window.

It was a gloomy, depressed region. The Dartmoor Road was nothing but a dark, muddy track through the woods. The coach came to a halt. As far as the eye could see, there wasn't a soul. She lowered the side window. "Send out a blast, Jack," said the voice. He blew on his trumpet. The coachman reined back the horses. First off, some dead leaves fell to the ground. Then they heard someone answer. Two men—one of them young, the other old—were running along the track. The young one reached the roadside, stopped, and doffed his hat. He could have been in his twenties, but he was extremely thin and worn out. His eyes looked like they were bruised. His face, skin plastered to his skull, was the face of death itself.

"Come closer, Christopher," said the voice. But he didn't budge. He gave a hint of a smile and turned his gaze toward the old man, who was just coming up. This one was even more extremely wretched, but he bore his wretchedness with pride and rage. Despite his peasant garb, he'd tied an old silk scarf, embroidered with dragons, around his neck. He hurried up to the coach. His eyes were very blue and hard.

"Come now, Ardan," said the voice, "here you are again, the way I don't want."

"I curse heaven, miss," the old man answered, as he took off his hat. "Soon I won't be able to hold back my desire to have done with this vale of tears."

Somebody must have signaled him that there was a person on top who could hear, because he glanced up at Herman, and then carried on in muffled tones. He was complaining. And he was being heard. Only now and then, the voice would say, "Yes, yes, my good man. Yes, Ardan." Then he fell silent.

"All right, all right," said the voice, "you know very well

he couldn't side with anyone but O'Brien. Would you have preferred him to be for Feargus O'Connor?"

"May that one be damned, miss. I beg your pardon."

"You curse everybody, Ardan."

"It's because I've nothing left in the world."

"You have Christopher."

"For how much longer, I wonder, miss."

"Oh, very well, Ardan," said the voice, "you are some kind of incurable old poet. William has done what he was supposed to do, and everything has turned out better than you could imagine. There's nothing make-believe about that."

"It's not that I'm pretending to be miserable, miss."

"That's not what I was trying to say, Ardan. All right, come closer. Come on, get up on the running board."

There was an affectionate and urgent note of command in the voice, and a small hand appeared, signaling him to come closer. The old man obeyed. He was pressed up against the coach. You couldn't make out what he was doing. Maybe he was putting something into the inside pocket of his jacket.

"We must be in pretty dire straits," he said.

But the friendly voice interrupted him. "You're an old fool, Ardan."

"It's true," said the old man, drawing back. "Can we expect to see you again soon, miss?"

"In less than a month, this time," she said.

The old man climbed up the embankment and headed toward the Dartmoor Road.

"Put your hat back on," said the voice.

"Thank you," he said, without turning around. He put his hat back on and headed into the woods.

The young man hadn't budged. He was gazing with ardor into the coach.

"Christopher, come on, don't be so shy, I'm not an evil spirit." But he didn't budge. Only his mouth had become mobile and passionate.

"We can leave, Jack," said the voice.

Herman had just been thinking that he'd wager a tidy sum...when he heard the voice again, in memory, as though it was still speaking. Meanwhile, the horses had gone back to trotting up the slope. In spite of the noise, he could still hear the voice. He really listened to it. This voice had soul. And the being reckless enough to have soul in our day and age, he thought, was a woman. Luckily for her, nine times out of ten, she was bound to run across fools. Even so, the men they'd met up with on the Dartmoor Road were no fools. Again, he saw the young man standing stock-still on the embankment, his gaze unwavering, his lips gradually becoming flushed and beautiful on his deathly face.

For a woman of such distinction, the terrible thing is to be a woman, that is to say, a thing that's pleasant to take possession of without worrying about painful consequences. Who still believes in painful consequences except for the woman who has no choice but to know they're real? Not all dandies are fools. Even if they are fools, they do have a certain something about them. There's so little character in the faces one sees in fashionable salons that a frock coat from Henley's or boots from Soupaut suffice to distract one's mind from the boredom. And there's so much generosity in that voice, she could go as far as to imagine soulfulness in someone who's nothing but a well-cut frock coat and a pair of highly polished boots. That someone will regard the best in her as nothing but trouble in the salons—as an obstacle to all the cunning maneuvers. He'll make fun of it. He'll try to destroy it. And, as for what's impassioned and honest in her look, he'll say to her straightaway: My dear, be less natural. We can see everything you're thinking. Don't bare your heart. People will take you for a little bumpkin.

Anyway, all of this is beside the point. Keep in mind that we've made some progress over nineteen centuries and that steam engines exist. If this imbecile is clever, as is often the case nowadays, he'll win her over. She'll lose her exceptionally rare quality. And since it's from that moment onward that she'll be successful, she'll say to herself: He's right: in fact, it was really easy not to be bored. Maybe she'll even acquire a taste for the frock coat. There won't be any more Dartmoor Roads. But, from this point on, she'll have to make sure she loses her own soul entirely. If she has even the tiniest bit of it left, it won't take long for her to despise the man she loves. What easy prey this woman must have been! And how easily some man must have made her miserable.

She can hardly be much older than the lad who was watching her with such sparkle in his eyes—the lad whose mouth became, all of a sudden, so beautiful. If I had as much soul as she does, I'd pretend to be a misanthrope. That would be the only way to save myself. With a little modesty, and a well-established reputation for being hard to get along with, I could still go on living. But I'm a man. A woman doesn't have the same possibilities. She's obliged, at every turn, to boldly expose all of her weakness, and there's no way to stop foolish men from wanting to get her in their grip and have a go at her. And sometimes it's impossible for her to defend herself—impossible even to want to defend herself—because of the fragrance of some hawthorn blossom, or because there's a warmish wind blowing, or because the gods are capable of wearing anybody down.

He felt like he knew her; that she must have a nature that

yielded itself up in advance and held nothing back. This soul, which floated on the surface of a voice, must surely trust in everyone. But did she know that, for the most part, even purity itself is impure? He recalled that he had seen something of her, after all: her delicate hand, which had gestured to the old man to come closer. She wears suede gloves, he said to himself. In a flash, this confirmed for him that this woman had already known suffering. She's already been very unhappy, he thought. What I was talking about just now—it must have happened. She must be sad, sad most of the time. She must already have experienced that pain of despising the person she loves. In spite of her youth, she can't have any hope left, except in what she must call her "wildest dreams." And even her dreams must make her suffer horribly, by reviving what she looks for without hope: what she thought she'd found, once, and what she came to realize was a huge mistake.

Now she has to mistrust herself. She can't have confidence in her own impulses anymore, and from moment to moment her own judgment must confirm the reasons for this mistrust. Her sadness must constantly make her reckon with what she's lost: above all, the joy of taking risks. She must consider herself to be inferior. No doubt she's capable of spending days on end sitting in an armchair, totally absent from where she appears to be. And she's become so attached to the places where she does go on such occasions, that she guards them with the utmost intensity from everyone else.

She's certainly well dressed, as if she wanted to make an impression. But her attention to her wardrobe hides her by making her resemble other women. Here, then, is the purpose of the suede gloves. There can't be any other reason for them. The tragedy of such an honest soul isn't even sublime; it's simply the tedium of living with mean-spirited people and of being constantly duped by them. Among them, coquetry has no appeal, unless you're soulless. And that voice of hers expresses all the subtle shadings of a heart deeply stirred by passion.

Not long after, he saw a large inn by the wayside. It was down at the bottom of the valley, where the road rejoined the Thames. He said to himself: The courtyard looks empty. We'll be alone, the two of us, in the dining room. I'll have to look at her. Maybe I'll even be forced to talk to her; in any case, I'll have to put on a brave front. I won't enter the inn. I'll ask the postilion if there's any way I can buy some food at the back door of the kitchen, and then I'll go and eat in the hay shed. I'll say that I don't feel well unless I'm out in the open air.

However, once the coach had come to a halt in the court-yard, he thought: I have to see her. He waited to find out which side of the coupé she was going to get down from. From his seat on the top deck, he climbed down on the op-posite side. He looked through the coach windows. He saw her. She was turning away from him and heading toward the door of the inn. The innkeeper was coming up to meet her. She must know him. She was giving him a friendly wave with her gloved hand. She was very elegant. Even in her ravishing dress, she had an extraordinary naturalness about her. Because she walked with a kind of boldness in every step, you wanted to be beside her to protect her, so that she might go on walking that way without running any risk.

She wasn't very tall; quite slender in her loose-fitting dress; and what gave onlookers an inexplicable jolt of pleasure was that in spite of the volume of her skirts, which were so supple and fitted her perfectly around the hips, you could sense her whole bodily presence inside. It should have been possible to see her hair or, at the very least, the shape of her head, but it was all hidden under a big, wide-brimmed silk hat. She casually took the arm of the innkeeper, who'd come forward to meet her. Leaning lightly on him, she went into the inn, crossing over the threshold with a quick, bird-like hop.

While the postilion was unhitching, Herman came up and asked if there was any way he could buy something to eat outdoors. It turned out to be very easy, because the postilion asked him if he was on his way back from the sea. Saying yes, Herman launched into telling him—in the blink of an eye, and almost without realizing it—a little tale, which must have been a pretty good one, since the other man stood there with his mouth hanging open, harness buckles in hand. At the same time, Herman was thinking: What on earth is this story all about? Why have I launched into spinning him a yarn, as if I wanted to make him my friend for life?

The postilion accompanied Herman all the way to the kitchen, and it was the postilion himself who ordered some food for his "mate who can't stand being pent up inside four walls." So Herman was able to buy, at little expense, a big chunk of pig's knuckle and some slightly dry bread pudding. And he made his way over to the hay shed. From where he was, he could see the big window of the dining room and, farther inside, the tall flames in the fireplace. They must have placed her table in front of the hearth. He saw her silhouette. Each time the tall flames died down, leaving shadow behind, something lingered within that shadow—something that kept on shining. And when the fire rekindled, the shining patch persisted, like a brighter core within the blaze. At last, he saw that it was straw-colored hair.

Abruptly, he felt a shiver run down his spine. It had just occurred to him that perhaps she was going to stay here, that she wouldn't carry on with the journey, that she'd reached her destination, that he'd never see her again. The familiarity she had with the innkeeper showed they were expecting her, they knew her. The baggage he'd seen them loading in London was still stowed away between the rear springs of the coach, but perhaps, in a minute or two, when the postilion had finished eating, he'd come and unfasten the big trunk and the two cases. Either that, or maybe this wasn't her baggage. Maybe she'd come here to wait for someone.

He suffered in solitude for more than an hour. He thought: I'll have to find a way to sleep out in the hay shed. I'll ask them at the kitchen. I'll say that I'll pay the same as I would for a room, but that I prefer to sleep outdoors. He was absolutely incapable of going into that inn and running the risk of encountering that woman on the stairs or in a corridor, of being forced to speak to her... even if it was only to excuse himself if they happened to meet in a doorway or to offer her the banister side of the staircase.

But the hay shed was the best place on earth. If, in the course of the afternoon, she were to come out, he'd see her. At last, the postilion came back to lounge around the coach, and he went up to the baggage. He checked the knots and cords, possibly because he was going to have to undo them. Herman didn't dare ask him anything. He offered him a little Manila cigar. He said to himself that now he really had to get the man interested in a good, long story, to charm him so he'd want to be helpful. But he was incapable of telling a story like the one he'd told when a new world was awakening inside of him. Now he was increasingly certain she was going to stay here. He could think of nothing else.

Finally, the postilion said he was going over to the stables for a little while. He wore a look of disappointment.

After two hours, which Herman spent pacing back and forth in front of the dining-room window without daring to look inside, they brought out fresh horses and started to harness. Soon the coachman climbed up onto his seat, and the groom tossed him the reins. She wasn't coming. He stood rooted to the ground, next to the coach. The postilion signaled to him that it was time. He was so visibly distracted, the postilion touched him on the arm. But she appeared in the open doorway, and she came forward, holding her wide-brimmed hat. And now, under the straw-colored hair, he saw her face: It was longish and pale. She had the cheekbones of a child. Next, she looked him in the eyes, and all he could remember was a color—a very lovely, unnameable color—and a doleful-looking mouth.

For the whole afternoon, while they were galloping along, he tried to picture that face again. But her gaze had erased it all. It was evening by the time they got past Marlowe. Then night fell, pitch-black and starless. In spite of the darkness, they kept the horses whipped into a gallop. A while later, when they must have been crossing a hill, the glare and then the flames of several large fires came into view, far down below. Herman asked what they were; he had no idea. It was a district known as the Four Fields, and here, during the day, they'd held a fair. The Mail stopped at the inn for the night. Lamps were burning under the canvas canopies, and the vendors were folding up the stalls. Cattle merchants were warming themselves around fires blazing in the fields.

The inn was full of people. Its open windows were steaming. The postilion carried the two cases. Herman followed. But when the woman entered the vestibule, it was obstructed by the heavy cloaks hanging from the racks on the walls. Servants in cherry-red livery passed through on the fly, carrying stacks of plates, shouting to make way. She drew back, and Herman instinctively moved close to her. She barely reached his shoulders. He was content to be strong and solidly built.

But there was really no more space in the dining room, except for a little spot next to the kitchen door, where it might be possible to set up a small table for the two of them, said a serving girl. So he felt frozen stiff all over again and couldn't stop himself from trembling. At this point, they were right up next to each other, standing between two rows of farmers who were sitting on benches. He'd turned his broad shoulders sideways to give her as much room as possible to get by, but even so, he was obliged to touch her, and he couldn't hide from her that he'd just trembled from head to foot. He pretended that someone had bumped into him.

She said, "Good, set up the table," and walked ahead down the long row of farmers, brushing their backs with her long dress. But she still had the same gait and held herself very erect. He followed her. He wasn't capable anymore of doing otherwise. He asked himself if it might not be better to leave, to get out of this place and take to the road. Still, he found himself sitting down across from her. He didn't dare look at her. He didn't know where to put his hands. He had a hard lump in his throat that he couldn't swallow. He tried to serve himself a drink. But suddenly the motion he made to take hold of the pitcher seemed extremely rash and he held back. As a result, he found himself with his hand up in the air, no longer knowing what to do, his mind a blank ... frozen from head to toe. The only thing he could think of was that she smelled of incense. He managed to will himself to grab hold of the pitcher and pour himself some water, very clumsily.

She had a scent similar to pine resin, but sugary, with a hint of vanilla. He tried two or three times to speak, to offer her a dish. But each time, the waft of incense—like a tepid breeze—robbed him of his powers. He thought: I must look at her. But he couldn't resolve to do it, not until he'd finally succeeded in saying "I beg your pardon, madame," in a voice he didn't recognize. He looked at her. Fortunately, at that particular moment, her eyelids were lowered, and her long, curved lashes appeared to be pressing onto her cheeks. Her eyebrows rose toward her temples; her long, narrow nose sloped down and there was something a little sly about it. But she lifted her eyes, and again he was dazzled by the unnameable color. He didn't have the presence of mind to avert his gaze right away, or to shut his own eyes. He remained stunned (his mouth could have been hanging wide open), and she was the one who looked away first. Immediately, he convinced himself that he had, in fact, remained there with his mouth wide open, like a total imbecile. Then he was so certain there was no longer any hope that he experienced a kind of calm. For a brief instant, there was no one across from him, not even an ordinary woman, and he was able to make a few controlled movements. He even risked looking at her.

He saw she had a slightly protruding forehead, with an almond-shaped swelling over the bridge of her nose, and that, despite all these signs of intelligence, her nostrils were exquisitely delicate. She was lightly and expertly made up. The skin of her cheeks was pearl-like behind a touch of rouge. Finally, when he was bold enough to note that her lips were full and glistening, he became conscious of the consummate beauty of this face. He experienced a feeling of deep peace-fulness, a relaxation of mind and body, a sense of well-being, as if life had become easy at last. It was a matter of comfort, however much he might not like the word. This intense beauty, so close to him, no longer made him freeze. On the contrary, it brought him to life, in a way he couldn't remem-ber ever having lived before. He was now capable of talking with ease, in a natural way. And when she stood up, acknowl-edging him with a slight movement of her head, he remained glued to his stool and said to her, "Good evening, madame," with a voice like a cadaver.

As soon as he was on his own, the rest of the crowd seemed to draw nearer. The rustic company was eating, drinking, smoking. There was muffled singing coming from the far end of the room. The maidservants shot out of the kitchen, like bullets, and flew back in. He had never expressed any-thing more beautiful, or more difficult, than that "Good evening, madame." He repeated it to himself, in a state of ecstasy, for what might have been half an hour. He was blind to everything... even a maidservant, barely more than a girl, in an unpleated skirt, who came in through the big doorway. Carrying neither plate nor pitcher, she went up to a group of farmers and started talking to them. It was only when she drew back that he recognized with a shock the straw-colored hair under her headdress. But she'd already left. He followed her. The vestibule was empty. He thought: No, I must be imagining I see her everywhere. He was going to climb the stairs, when a chambermaid, coming out of the laundry room, passed by him and went on ahead. In her hand she was carrying the stays for the bodice of a petticoat and, folded over her arm, that dress, which he easily recognized. She stopped on the first floor while he carried on; he heard her knock gently on a door; the voice asked who was there. The servant said, "It's the dress," and the person inside opened the door.

All of this was difficult to account for. For more than an hour, he had no trouble coming up with explanations. Each explanation was conclusive, but then he would come up with an even more conclusive explanation. At last he said to himself that, really, all of this was difficult to account for. He remained wide-eyed, stark naked on his bed of hay, ever so happy, ever so peaceful, seeing clearly, but not fully understanding anything... other than the beautiful face. It must have been late; there were no more noises from the inn; outside, two men went on singing, trying to harmonize their voices. Herman wasn't sleeping. He felt flushed with a sort of victory, similar to the one of the past spring when he invincibly fended off thousands of men and finally crushed them beneath his feet of flowers. Little by little, he started to fall asleep. But repeatedly, as he was about to drop off—just as he was about to unmoor himself and surrender his powers—he woke up with a start, as though he was unwilling to enter this realm that eradicated everything.

There was no more sound. Like little red birds, the last flickerings from the fireplace flitted against the windowpanes. He thought: Tomorrow, I have to talk to her. It was the easiest thing in the world; all he had to do was go up and talk to her. It was so easy, it was already said and done. So he went to sleep.

On awakening, he remembered that he'd touched her the evening before, when both of them were standing between the farmers' benches, and the serving girl was setting up the little table beside the kitchen door. At that moment when he'd shivered, he was pressed so closely against her, her chest was touching the length of his arm. And as she was breathing in, perhaps (he thought wildly) her breast was touching me. He imagined her breast, warm, naked, sensitive, in the shadow of her corset. After that, there was no way in the world he could talk to her.

But while they were harnessing the horses, he came up to her abruptly and said, "I could tell it was you last night, you'll never be able to disguise yourself; you—" He stopped himself. She's gone very pale. She's going to fall down. She's no longer breathing. He sees her eyes. They're the color of tobacco, with green highlights. But she closes them and says, in a hushed voice, "You too, you disguise yourself poorly." And the gravity of her voice is so hard to bear, that he answers immediately, he almost shouts, "But I'm not disguised!"

There must have been some misunderstanding. She looked him over from head to foot. Now she was on the verge of smiling: He was so distressed!

"These are the clothes I'm used to," he said. "I really am a sailor, though it's been some years since I've been to sea. I dressed this way to feel more at ease." And, since she was smiling, he went on to add, "But what did you find wrong, I mean, badly disguised, about all of this?"

"Your cigars," she said.

He looked at the one between his fingers, which was still smoking.

"They're little Pireïrras," she said, "from the Compania di Charutos. I know them. My husband used to smoke them, back when he imitated everything my brother did. They're not sailors' cigars."

"It's true," said Herman. "But sailors do smoke them in the parts of the world where they're made. That's where I picked up the habit."

"So you really are a sailor?" There was still a note of anxiety in her voice.

"I really am one, and I can tell you my name, to clear up any doubt."

She agreed, with a nod.

"My name is Melville. Herman Melville."

She considered the name for a moment in silence, and then she asked if he was the writer from America. He said yes. Her smile now became genuine; a bloom came over her lips, and her expression relaxed.

"Did that put you more at ease?"

"Could you tell that I wasn't?"

"You were pale and out of breath, and I thought you were going to faint."

"Even so, I felt like I was putting on a brave front," she said, as if talking to herself.

Indeed, she looked like she was drawing on all of her shaken resources, passionately, honestly, and without an ulterior motive.

"What are you afraid of?" he said.

"I can't tell you anything. Except that it's a very good thing for me that you are Herman Melville." She touched his arm and left her hand there, as though she intended to lean on him. "You've been scaring me since yesterday." And, as he gave a questioning look, "I'll explain," she said. "Come on, let's climb up now. Yes, I'm going to ride up top with you. The coupé is too crowded today."

This whole exchange took place while heavyset farmers were getting into the carriage and the postilion and the coachman were loading parcels and baggage. She and Herman were sitting on the front bench, directly above the coachman's seat. And so, barely covered by the big hood of the coach, they launched headfirst together, at once, into the vast, wooded countryside and into the sky. They were passing through the forests at a gallop, at the height of the heavy limbs of the trees. Two farm women were seated next to them, as well as a man, who must have been a shepherd, dressed in a sheepskin vest with the wool facing out.

They were squeezed up against each other. As they were settling in, she'd put her hand under her dress to gather up the hoops of her petticoat. When she'd seated herself beside him, he'd seen the outline of her knees appear under the loosened fabric. And now she was touching him; and he was touching her, with his hip and his leg.

Morning was brushing the land the way green willow boughs brush the water's surface. Ripples of liquid light were spreading out across the meadows and the woods, and splashing back as gold dust against the grass stems and the branches. Because of the noise of the wheels, it wasn't possible to talk. But from time to time, when a new range of sunlit hills emerged from the mist, the two of them looked at each other.

The country they'd entered into was mountainous and harsh. Several times already the horses had slowed to a walking pace. Finally, as they left the valley, the coach started up a longer slope. At this point, they had to give the horses a rest. They came to a stop, and everyone got down onto the road. He walked beside her; she'd gathered up her long, supple dress in her hand.

"Where are you headed?" she said.

"I don't know. I'm going wherever my fancy takes me."

"Knowing that would have made things a lot clearer to me. I would actually have been able to stop myself from being scared."

"Did you think I was a highwayman?"

She smiled, and her face turned childlike and very pure, as if not of this world. "No, instead I took you for a constable."

"I didn't know they dressed like this."

"They dress themselves in all sorts of ways, even in clouds. A poet ought to know. Remember Lady Macbeth? Why did you leave on a Tuesday?"

"Because it was on a Tuesday that I thought of leaving."

"But you were going somewhere?"

"Why, yes, certainly. And you?"

"I always have specific destinations."

"Then where, very specifically, are you going, my lady?"

"You're playing a game. Let's say I was on my way to Monmouth."

"This isn't a game. I too am on my way, very specifically, to Monmouth. It's strange, isn't it?"

"What will be strange," she answered, "is when you agree to tell me, without lying, why you took the carriage from Gray's Inn on a Tuesday."

"I can sense," he said, "that we've come to the very heart of the matter. I never lie, but if I did, I certainly wouldn't lie about anything this important. I took the carriage from Gray's Inn because it was going in the direction I was headed."

"No, sir, you very specifically took the one that was *not* going where you were headed. On Tuesdays, the mail coach going directly to Bristol leaves from Hatton Garden. That's the day when the one from Gray's Inn makes a detour through Four Fields. What do you say to that?"

"I have to say that they failed to inform the United States of this, my dear lady. Always this disdain and indifference on the part of Europe toward us poor Americans. We knew nothing about it in Massachusetts. Imagine that."

"It's easy for you to act smart, but what should I say? I take this coach on Tuesdays to be alone. And here I am, very specifically, with a Redskin on my hands! You were neither a merchant, a farmer, nor a regular at the inn... not even a normal man. I smiled at you last night, and you sat there like a block of wood."

"When?"

"And you have to ask? Admit it, poets do the most outrageous things without batting an eye."

"In that case, you must be a kind of great poet," said Herman. "But come on, they're calling us. We have to get back to our perch."

They'd reached a mournful, treeless plateau. They started to drop passengers off here and there: in villages, on farms, at cottages. Even out in the open country, the carriage would stop, and the person would get down and make their way, alone. There were no dwellings in sight for miles around, either in one direction or in the other. Little by little, the carriage got lighter. Though the roads were bad in this high country, they were empty, so they launched onto them at full gallop. The ground was soft. Now the carriage's wheels and the horses' shoes made only muffled sounds.

In the distant, motionless reaches, Herman saw an extraordinary light. It transformed the misty crepe of the far-flung woods into lamb's fleece. Rust-colored pasturelands covered the earth like wool carpets. So now Herman started to talk about the world that lay before them. He rolled up the sky, from one edge to the other, as though it were made out of colored silk. And, for a brief moment, there was no more sky. Then, after an interval of four hoofbeats at a gallop, he rolled the sky open again, but now it had turned into a huge skin, tightly enclosing earth's arteries and veins.

Autumn storms were slumbering along the perimeter of the plateau. He pointed out an indentation in the sky, between two snowy masses of cloud. It was in the shape of a leaf; it was a nocturnal green, and through the color one saw the infinite depths appear.

"Do you remember having held a bay leaf in your hands?"

"Yes."

"Do you remember the color of the leaf?"

"Yes."

"As dark as night?"

"Yes."

"But green, all the same."

"Yes."

"A kind of green that seems to come from very far away, that rises up through the dark color, as though the leaf itself were a world?"

"Yes."

"As if chasms were opening up in the leaf?"

"Yes."

And so, suddenly, she had that indentation of the sky in her hand; she felt the chasms in the sky grow deeper in her hand; she saw them right before her eyes. The world wasn't the same anymore: She knew that she was very small, that the sky was infinite; but now it was she who was infinite, and the sky very small. Simply because she had once held in her hand a bay leaf, whose flesh is the same as that vast, dusty cloud of dark, green sand: the night. And above all, because a voice had just named it for her, had fused the two images, had shed light on them.

He made the woods come closer. Had she ever seen a wood the way he was making her see it?

"No."

He revolved it for her, turned it upside down, turned it inside out: the eastern edge, the western edge, the mysteries of the north and the south, the moss, the fungus, the scent, the color.

"Had you seen it?"

"No."

"Have you seen it?"

"Yes."

He sent the woods back to where they'd come from. They retreated, shrank, lay down again at the rim of the horizon. Had she really noticed the birches with their horsehide bark?

"No."

He summoned the birches. And the birches came. She felt them, not just right next to her, as if she was in an ordinary field and had leaned against one; she felt them in her heart. He took hold of the tree with its sticky sap, its sound, its smell, its shape, its leaves, its four seasons, and ... there was no telling how he did it, but she felt the tree in her heart and, at the same time, she could touch the bark. She'd never had a sensation as pleasurable as that of her empty hand imagining it was touching the birch and sensing, through it, the things he was saying.

He said to her, "Look at the water in those little marshes." The water moved closer, with its rushes, its tadpoles, its frogs, its moorhens, its ducks, its kingfishers, all of its bird feathers, its cottony, flowering canes, its muck, its smell of rain. "Hold on, let's stay with the smell of rain, you'll see."

He sustained everything else, only he lowered its register, as if he were lifting off, ever so slightly, the pressure from the pedal of a big cathedral organ. The birds, the fish, the frogs, the canes, the whole of the muck-filled marsh droned together as a basso continuo accompaniment from the vaulted recesses of the earth; and he made the smell of the rain sing as a fugue. All the old showers that had slanted down, through the ages, over the whole face of the earth, rose up again like stalks in an enormous field of wheat. She remembered the rains of her childhood, Sunday afternoons in the attic with the smell of rats, old installments of tales of chivalry, movements from clocks that no longer kept time and clockwork toys whose movements were broken, the chests covered with goatskin, the smell of rain-washed roofs, and the rain falling over the silent town, where everyone was at church.

He made her come to life, no longer as a woman sitting beside a man on the top deck of the Bristol Mail but as an absolute ruler of the weather; he made her come alive in her own domain. She could plainly feel that he was granting her his own world. She realized that when he was mute and unable to move (as he was yesterday), when he was apart from her (yesterday, for example, when she didn't know him yet, when he was keeping quiet up here, and she was all alone down below in the coupé), when he wasn't in touch with anyone else, he still saw the world in the same way he was seeing it and naming it now. He could summon the rain for himself alone.

Now he'd summoned the rain for himself and for her. He was enabling her to share his private world, which, in a completely natural way, became her world. Her own world, so private to her that she often blushed at everything this man seemed to know about her: the whole of her secret life. She remembered rash impulses, from her girlhood, that had never escaped the confines of her heart, and here, he—a man unknown to her yesterday—was talking to her about them.

Be gone, smell of rain. Go back underground, stored-up reservoir of showers.

Look: The marshes rose up. She could see through the waters, as though she were looking through colored glass. The wool of the fields wrapped itself around her inflated dreams of chivalry. The autumn meadows carpeted all the childhood rooms where she'd lain in bed with fever. The forests, the woods, the groves, the big shade trees—torn from the ground by their resident flocks of birds—were flying around her, like the shawls they wrapped her with when they left on holidays, in the middle of the night, in her grandfather's dogcart; it even seemed to her that a few little clumps of that soil that clings to tree roots had fallen onto her dress. She made a motion to brush them away with her hand. At last, when they reached the midday stopover, as she set foot on the ground, she said, "I beg of you, give me your arm, please, I am drunk."

They ate in silence, at the same table.

"My God," she said, "you've gone very pale all of a sudden. Behind your beard, you look as if you're made of wax!"

He'd just been thinking that he had no one in the world but her. He looked at her, without answering. She thought: I was wrong to talk to him about his paleness. He must have one of those Oriental fevers that recur in fits and starts. He might have to recover at an inn. I could take care of him. He thought: She's here, but she can leave. She'll go her own way, if not today, then tomorrow. Maybe I'm going to lose her.... Why say "maybe"? Without a doubt, I'm going to lose her.

He imagined a world—unlike the real one—where he wouldn't lose her. The air would have to be a wall, he thought, invisible but solid, and I'd have to know about a door. He imagined he was opening this door, and on the other side, there was a different world. He would say, "Come, my lady." She came. He closed the door behind them. And thus, the two of them were in a land, an unimaginable land, where he was the only one who knew her, and she knew no one but him. The two of them, inseparable.

Between Henley and Cricklade, the Mail stopped for the night. They weren't going to press on past the Queen Elizabeth Inn. They got there at close to four o'clock in the afternoon. The road to Cricklade was too long and ran through uninhabited moors. On many occasions, there'd been problems with broken axles. Passengers had been obliged to warm themselves all night around brushwood fires, without a bite to eat. Oh my! The postilion and the coachman couldn't stop talking in the most dismal terms about these makeshift encampments. They put a lot of stress on "without a bite to eat" and insisted that, toward four in the morning, "even the brushwood had started to run short." What's more, the distance was too great for the horses.

The truth was that Jeremiah—the owner of the Queen Elizabeth—gave, as they say, "a certain percentage" to the operator of the Mail. As for the postilions and the coachmen, they'd say that their "one for the road" in the morning wasn't really that important; they were more partial to their nightcap. In other words, when their workday was done, they preferred to knock back a glass in peace and, whenever possible, for free. In this regard, Jeremiah was generous. And he was kind to everyone. It wasn't unpleasant to halt during the daytime. There was still a good hour of sunlight. As a matter of fact, said Jeremiah, for the most part the gentlemen travelers thank me for giving them the chance, like this, to stretch their legs.

The area wasn't particularly impressive. By dusk that evening, it looked to be an unbroken, naked moorland, hemmed in on every side by the encroaching mist. But the ground was meadow-like, thick as a wool carpet, reddish-brown, and strewn with autumn crocuses. Your footsteps sank into the springy softness.

"Look," said Herman, "this is exactly the kind of meadow the English love to walk on. Come, let's go for a stroll."

"Wait a moment," she said, "I'm not a member of the first night watch. I don't climb up on deck as soon as the bell sounds. I have to get myself ready." She pointed out the hoops of her petticoat. Her dress clung tightly around her childlike body. With her beautiful hair alone, you might have mistaken her for a young boy, but her very feminine bust, and this long dress, which tumbled to the ground and bunched back up in puffs, made her seem like a sort of a cherub, one you would set on a pedestal.

"Women are always having to get themselves ready," he said. "You're fine just like that. You could pass for the Virgin of Lima. Nothing could be more fitting. You're completely ready. Come on, we're going on a magic stroll."

So she gave the hoops to the boy who was carrying her baggage, and she gathered her dress up in big handfuls. "All right, let's go," she said.

"Here we are," he said. (After a hundred yards, they were hidden in the mist.) "Look. Everything has disappeared, there's nothing left: no carriage, no inn, no people. Forward, march!"

"Look at you now, sailor, full of swagger. Don't forget that I'm walking with fifteen feet of fabric around my legs. Forward, then, but not too fast."

"Try a little harder. I'm not giving you my arm, because you have to be really lost. Are you really lost?"

"I'm perfectly lost. My dress is wrapped around me like a layer of bark. Five minutes from now, I'll be lost and marooned at the same time, like a tree in the middle of a field."

"All right then, everything's going well. This is exactly what was required. ... When my mother lost a couple of pennies (she was a remarkable person, my mother), when she lost a couple of pennies, she used to say—of course, only after she'd searched everywhere, sometimes for weeks—when she finally gave up, she used to say, 'They haven't been lost for everyone.' When I was a little boy, this way of seeing things had a great influence on me. I assure you, if you'd known my mother (I wish you had known my mother), you'd have been convinced, like me, that when it came to pennies—their zoology, their anatomy, their astrology—my mother knew everything. She was the Cassandra of pennies. She had the gift of seeing their future through thin air. I've wondered for a long time. ... (Could you take a few more steps, in spite of it all? We don't need to have the mist, but if we are going to have it, at least it should be thick.) For a long time, I've wondered where that place was, where even my mother couldn't find two pennies. Because it was real, and from the moment she said so, there was no reason to doubt it might also be a place where people could hide. Have you never longed for a place where you could escape from worldly powers, a kind of refuge, like the Merovingian churches? Now, take my arm.

"I've often thought: Someday it could happen, while you're walking along any kind of a road, that you cross over a mysterious barrier, without suspecting it. It looks to me like this is exactly what you and I have just done, at the very same moment. Together we put pressure on a kind of membrane in the air, and it burst when we passed through. Look out! From now on it's just the two of us, alone, inseparable. It made a sound you could barely perceive, but didn't you hear it too? I wish you'd answer me. No, don't let go of my arm.

I beg your pardon. I thought you wanted to let go. Yes, lean on me as hard as you want to. And don't say a word. I believe, in fact, that we've just crossed over to the other side.

"I don't recognize the path anymore, and it winds around a hill we've never seen. Behind it, there's an unfamiliar town. Do you like mountains? The town sits on the slopes of this mountain. The sky is absolutely blue. It's ridiculous to say so, but that's how it is. High up, right where the moon rises, the frozen peaks—they're as sharp as wolves' teeth—are whistling in the wind. Listen! I agree. It's difficult to believe it's the wind that's making that sound. That whistling doesn't remind us of anything. We've never heard the wind sounding like that before, have we? The trees over there, the hedges, the fields, none of this reminds us of any trees or fields we've already seen. No, none of it has any connection with our memories, and our memories are fading away. We've never seen anything like what we're seeing now, together. And so, it's completely natural that the life we've lived up until now is fading fast.

"But as we've been moving along, the mountains have circled around the sky. Now they've closed up again, behind us. They're the Negro mammies. Oh, these mammies have been around a lot longer than the ones you see in Provincetown, puffed up in silks like balloons, with their tubular white head cloths, busy looking after the young gentlemen. No, these Negro mammies are stark naked, and they're playing this way so they can slowly gather their little ones in their arms. Oh, for them it's the greatest game in the world!

"They have a word that means 'nevermore,' and that's what they call the game. If you think about it, it's really clever. It wraps the fulfillment of all human desires into one single desire, and it does this so well, it must have come down to us from the beginning of time. It has to have been the first, great, mournful game that Adam and Eve played on the first beach where they landed after they left the earthly Paradise. You won't rid me of the notion that it's the ocean waves that teach this to the Negro mammies, during the afternoons when the water turns the pages of the big blue book, over and over, one after the other, at the water's edge.

"The black child is standing there, in front of his crouching mother. She reaches out her arms, and then she doesn't move. It looks like she's motionless, just the way it looked like the mountains were motionless a moment ago. But, imperceptibly, her arms move forward and wrap around the child. He waits, all atremble. He's afraid, and he's full of joy, which makes him ticklish. At one and the same time, he has the desire to take off and . . . oh, the desire that it should happen! That what should happen? All of it. . . . He doesn't know. And he waits there, standing still, while his swollen heart beats with all its might inside his chest.

"Then the hands slowly close behind his back. At last! Ah, at last! Happiness holds him captive, and he buries his head in the mother's bosom. He squashes his nose right up against her black breasts, he shuts his eyes, and, with a kind of rumbling hangover—heavy, drunken, lost, all of it!—he leaves the world behind, far, far away. . . . And he's saved! Naked nevermore, alone nevermore, weak nevermore, cold nevermore, all of it nevermore . . . except for drunken happiness. And this is the way the mountains have closed behind us. Nevermore! If we wanted to get out of here now, on every side we'd be risking our lives along walls of ice.

"But the town—did you ever play with building blocks when you were young? All right, the houses are like those blocks that used to amuse you, and they rise from terrace to terrace on the mountainside. There's a wonderful silence. Once in a while, the black water flowing out of the glaciers forms a little waterfall between two mica rocks; otherwise, you can go for a long time and hear nothing at all. Then, high above, or far below, somebody opens a door to come out and warm themselves in the sun, on a doorstep made of matted grass. And there you have the town! Oh, I know it, because I've hungered for it for so long! The men and the women of the whole world have built this town inside themselves, step by step, stone by stone, flower by flower. And they've built this living mountain, a mountain that can play the old trick of 'surprising happiness' or the game of 'nevermore.' But since the whole world is stronger than a Negro woman (who knows, maybe not? it might be better to say: since the desires of the whole world are stronger than a Negro woman), rather than gather us in its arms, it holds us tight with these glaciers, which we can't even imagine. And it really is 'nevermore.' Because everyone knows, by instinct, that happiness is a necessity. Without it, ah! . . . . And we're so adept at losing it. If it doesn't make itself inevitable, with the power of an insurmountable peak, we're forever trying to flee from it . . . like water, through the deepest valleys, the darkest caves, the foulest-smelling badger holes . . . to slide our dead weight down there, to drain away and disappear, effortlessly, down the slope.

"But now, happiness has taken us by surprise. It's hemmed us in with its wolf-toothed mountains. You know, over the course of thousands and thousands of years of human desires, it's done things in a peculiar way, but it's done them well. So much for the heart. The mind, now, the mind is an entirely different matter. The mind talks. The heart, on the other hand, doesn't say anything. It's there, in your chest, like a pair of little clogs. And it goes clip-clop, clip-clop, clip-clop along a road it travels without a word. The mind doesn't go anywhere. It's stuck where it is, and it keeps on chattering endlessly. It asks questions.

"By the way, do you know the meanest trick you can play on someone's mind? It's to overwhelm it with wonders. You have to do what we did to one of our shipmates on our way home from the Bahamas. We were sailing along with pennants flying and the holds full. The ship was like one big sofa: There was nothing left to do but eat, drink, sleep, sing... and take it easy. This mate of ours—I think it was all the lazing about that got him stirred up—he goes and starts recalling that he was a doctor of something or other, I can't remember what; or that he'd had a mate who was a doctor; or that he himself had served as a footman at a college of doctors; or something along those lines. In any case, there he was doctoring us, redoctoring us, and indoctrinating us.

"And, once again, it was a Negro who did the trick. He brought him one of those gorgeous, repulsive creatures you can haul out of the sea—as many as you like, if that's what you happen to be interested in: one of the most beautiful and, at the same time, one of the most repulsive things in the world. Picture something soft, moist, transparent, formless... and in the middle of all this formlessness, two eyes: two very beautiful eyes, completely human, with lids, with long, soft lashes, beautiful, golden irises, and beautiful whites— a little bluish, like aristocrats have, eyes like fathers sometimes have, eyes with a reproachful look, one that says, 'Now then, boy, is *this* how you squander your time?' Well, the Negro slapped this thing right onto the knees of the other man (who was sitting at the foot of the mainmast) and then he walked away, upright, bracing himself, because we were heading into a bit of a fresh breeze. He walked away with determination, as though the matter was settled. And the matter was settled. The other sailor looked at those beautiful eyes, which were, believe me, like a poet's eyes, but a gigantic poet's eyes (the creature had been hauled up from a depth of who knows how many fathoms). I'm telling you, he looked at those ever so beautiful eyes, floating in their mass of jelly, and after that, he shut his trap for the rest of the voyage. Mysteries are mysteries.

"Imagine if, after having seen the town on the mountain, we were to say to each other, 'This is all very fine, but let's go and get something to eat.' (One's mind is perfectly capable of saying this; it's the heart that revels in the silence of the huge meadowlands down below the glaciers.) We arrive at the inn. You say to me, 'Don't you think the people here seem terribly strange?' I say to you, 'Why, yes, they really are. I hadn't noticed it until just now. Hold on.' And I ask them, 'Where is our table, and what will we be having to eat this evening?' I ask them in the most natural way I can, you know, looking playful, rubbing my hands together in anticipation. I try to make it seem like I don't see their long mustaches, which hang all the way down to the ground. They've made knots and braids in them, so they won't get in their way. But, all the same, they are, you might say, tangled up in their mustaches from head to foot. And in spite of the fact that I've spoken to them, they look at me, and they look at you, and they look at each other... and they don't answer. Then they do answer, but now it's incomprehensible: a sort of mustache-talk that nobody can understand. You say to me.... Well, no. You don't say anything to me. You drop your arms in defeat. We do our utmost to make them understand: This is an inn, here's a table, we want to eat.... No. I show them with sign language: We want to eat.... No. So then they start looking at us with their eyes popping out like marbles. They're munching on their mustaches while they check us out in every detail. They're munching ferociously on their mustaches!

"Then I say to you, 'Let's get out of here. There must be a town over there. Let's go.' We go. On the way, I stop for a moment to point out to you that the path to the town is really lovely.

"You speak English. I speak English. But, when it comes to English-speakers in this particular world, there's only us. We can't be apart anymore. The path is very lovely. But in the town, it's the same thing: full of mustachioed men. What in heaven's name have we gotten ourselves tangled up in? Really, things weren't this way just a short time ago. We got off the Bristol Mail. We set out on foot through a meadow—the kind the English are so fond of walking on—and look at us now!... Yes, but what about the membrane in the air, the one that burst when we passed through? What on earth are we going to be able to do now? I don't mean only for this evening but for the rest of our lives. Because it's settled: We're in this now for good. What's more, this town is quite lovely. But we're going to have to do something to survive. For my part, I'm a good sailor. But if it comes to sailing, I'll be leaving you behind. And that's out of the question. And, besides, do they even have a sea, these people? What do you say about that?"

"Like you," she says, "I'm starting to wonder. What are we going to do?"

"Ah, so you see, it isn't funny at all."

"Well, all right, I have a pretty good idea," she says. "Desperate ills call for desperate remedies. I'm going to go and find the Grand Turk. Surely there must be a Grand Turk in this country?"

"What? You wonder if there's a Grand Turk? But the place is full of them. They're all Grand Turks."

"No, but I mean the grandest of all. The one and only Turk, if you prefer."

"All right. And then what will you do with your one Grand Turk?"

"Women know very well how to make use of Grand Turks. I'm going to dance before the Grand Turk. I hope he'll understand that."

"As a matter of fact, if he has a pair of eyes, I think he will understand. But what will that gain us?"

"Some cash."

"Hey now, Virgin of Lima, I don't like this idea at all—of you dancing before the Grand Turk."

"Why is that, sailor?"

"Well, that's the way it is. Find something else."

"All right then, I could sell myself for his harem."

Night had fallen. She pressed her arm a little harder against Herman's. "Let's go on walking a little longer in your town of the mist, if you like," she said. "Unfortunately, I know they speak English very well back at the Queen Elizabeth."

———

The following day they took the eight o'clock stagecoach and by noon they were at Cricklade. They wouldn't be departing again until six the next morning. The town was cold and dark. They went out into the fields. They came across a big stand of tall broom grass. "Look," said Herman, "this too is a kind of town, with streets and squares. I used to pretend to get lost in thickets like this when I was a boy. Come on inside."

They made their way in through the heavy stems, along corridors of a kind, and they actually reached the center of the thicket: a small green chamber, carpeted with very soft grass not yet touched by the night frosts.

"Let's stay here," she said. "Lie down next to me and listen: My name is Adelina White. Since I'm talking about myself, let's make the most of it. This is something I thought about all day yesterday. Take a pencil and write down my address. I'd be so happy if you'd write to me when we've gone our separate ways."

"It's true," he said, "we are going to be separated, in spite of the land of mist and the town on the mountain."

"In spite of the land of mist and the town on the mountain, yes. Write this down: Adelina White, 16 Seething Road, Leeds. Hand me your pencil. Give me your address."

"Herman Melville, 184 Mashpee Avenue, Massachusetts."

"There we go. So my name is Adelina White. Are you aware of what happened in England last year?"

"In what regard?"

"I'm going to tell you. Do you remember the famine of '46?"

"Very well. I saw the boats loaded with emigrants arriving in our country, and I brought them a good many kettles of soup myself."

"Nothing has changed."

"I assumed so. An entire population doesn't stop dying of hunger all at once."

"No, but it stops faster if you think about the starving bellies and work to fill them, instead of spending your time philosophizing about the doctrines of Adam Smith and Ricardo. I know that thousands of English men and women were in agony because they knew what was happening in the Irish cottages. You saw the boatloads of emigrants; we saw the cartloads of corpses thrown into the pits. Still, in spite of everything, for two years the English merchant ships never stopped sailing away with England's rich harvests of wheat, to sell them in foreign markets. And this at the very height of the potato famine, when the wretched Irish peasants were weeping with hunger, perched on the gates of their rotten fields.

"The government ministers feared the objections of the economists: It seemed that intervention by the state ran counter to the laws those gentlemen had cleverly devised. By the time the government thought of doing something, England's wheat was far away and feeding foreign mouths. The government arranged for wheat to come from the Indies, but they put its distribution into the hands of common merchants, who made a fortune through speculation.

"Humans are the weakest creatures in the world because they're intelligent. Intelligence is, by definition, the art of turning a blind eye. If you want to remedy an ill, you can't turn a blind eye. For me, in this instance (choose your own, according to your nature), it's a twenty-year-old boy who's dying of starvation. He was born to live and to love.

"No dying person behaves better than someone who's starving to death: He doesn't speak, he doesn't moan... he dies, without making a fuss, lying on the ground.... And most of the time he hides his face, as though he were ashamed. To him you can turn a blind eye the most easily. But have the courage (or the sentimentality, if you like) to lift that head up and look at that face, and you'll say to yourself: This man has to eat. He has to eat immediately.

"Then you won't think anymore about selling. You'll think about giving. Which is the very opposite of the economists' laws, and not 'intelligent' at all, I'll grant you that. Sentimentality."

"If I'm not saying anything," said Herman, "it's because I'm listening to you very intently."

"That's all. As you can see, I don't know anything about politics. Last year there was the meeting of the Chartists at Kennington Common. I don't know which of them was right, Feargus O'Connor or William Smith O'Brien. All I know is, they took O'Brien prisoner in a cabbage field and condemned him to death. My husband defended him. I realize that telling you this is hardly an advertisement for the lawyer in the case. Still, there's nothing to reproach him with. He did what he could. It wasn't much, but he did it. Besides, the sentence was commuted. I don't know to what extent he might consider it one of his personal successes. He's an unfeeling man."

"What are you thinking about?" said Herman, after a brief silence.

"I'm thinking about your glaciers, from yesterday evening," she said, "the ones that hold the town on the mountain tightly in their arms. I'm accustomed to glaciers that offer no refuge. O'Brien's father is on Dartmoor."

"And that young man who looked at you with so much soul?"

"That's his other son, Christopher. I run contraband wheat for the starving people of Ireland. At the very least, I act as the go-between, because Christopher said I looked like a bird and could get past the fences. At the Four Fields fair, I was supposed to meet the man who'll drive the carts to the landing, near the mouth of the Severn. I did meet him. I'll be leaving you tomorrow evening."

There was a very long silence.

"I'm a country girl," she said.

"I could tell," he said.

"Is it obvious?"

"No, it's a feeling. I knew, even before I saw you—after I heard you talking to old O'Brien. I'm a man who's tangled a few times, face-to-face, with at least three of the four elements, and there's only one thing that gets you through: the soul. Elsewhere, you can get along without it; but there, no. There was an earthiness in your voice. I wondered how all of that could fit in with genteel society (I'd seen your gloved hand), and then I didn't ask myself any more questions."

"If you knew the house I was born in, you'd be astonished by my dresses and my hands."

"I'm not easily astonished," he said, "especially when I see things that are clear and easy to understand."

"On an old engraving of my village," she said, "you can see my house on the side of the hill. I've drawn a heart around those walls and some of the fields where I spent my days. It's not so very long ago that I drew that heart. One evening, just like any other, in the house where I live now, I suddenly felt the desire, you see, to trace the shape of a heart. Yes, to watch my fingers draw that shape with the quill. The line that starts from the middle, swells out as it rises, fills with tenderness, and then curves down, still inflated, to come together at the bottom tip. On an ordinary evening, with my husband in his usual place in his armchair, with my child—I have a four-year-old son—with my son upstairs in his bedroom, the clock ticking, the fire in the chimney, the tranquility... I felt the urge to draw a heart. Sometimes you feel the need to make sure that certain things exist. As soon as I was in my bedroom, I opened the drawer where I kept the old engraving, and that's where I drew the heart: around my old house.

"It was a farm with worn-out soil, but the Whites (that's my maiden name, the one I gave you just before) had made it into a wonderful refuge. Don't go thinking I'm soft and sensitive. I'm tough enough. That was a strict household. There were five of us children: I have three brothers and a sister. The oldest of the lot, Harold, isn't funny—a word you're fond of. If I'm telling you this, it's because I was talking just a moment ago about my husband in his armchair.

"My father used to leave in the morning, on horseback, with two plowboys. The three horses would set out, at a walk, to plow the uplands. As for little girls, you can't expect them not to be women already. The youngest of the lot was Pitt, a boy who would have won your approval, who would win it still. Harold adores children. He's always looked at them with a strict, probing eye, but at the same time, with such a peaceful expression on his face that they come up and touch his hand. My sister and Pitt and I used to say, 'Harold is a healer.' The fact that children understood this instinctively (I was seven, and my sister was nine), and that Harold would actually become a healer, in accordance with the wishes of the whole family, this will show you, better than anything, how all of us used to think along the same lines. And it will tell you about the character of our father, who would head out to the distant fields every day without saying a word but seeing everything.

"I didn't say 'doctor' (I'm thinking about your 'doctor' from yesterday evening). Nothing was 'doctoral' with Harold, and nothing is now (he has a clinic for children, in a suburb of Birmingham). No, to put it simply, with his sternness and his silence, he's a healer. He dispenses healing, because you see a heart drawn around him. And children see it much better than everybody else. He understood that, with children, he had the best chance to heal—above all, with poor children, who yearn for mysteries and never get to see any. So they get to see one, at last, in this man. And they recover. Or at least, from then on, they're ready to recover.

"Pitt became his assistant. Pitt is delightful; I love Pitt. I like them all, but I love Pitt. He used to have a completely hilarious way of falling on his...yes...and afterward he would come up to you, aching all over, sincere as can be, and ask if it hadn't hurt *you*! It looked like a joke, but he'd be excruciatingly concerned with your hands, your feet, your flanks, your crown of thorns. He'd shout, 'Watch out! They're going to bring you a sponge soaked in vinegar.' He's always worried about the harm that other people can do to you through him. He's three years younger than me. He looks like me. I love him.

"I didn't know my other brother very well. Nobody else did, for that matter. He's the perfect vessel for what people in our part of the country call 'the silence of the Whites.' Of the male Whites...because, here and now, right in front of you, this representative of the female Whites is talking. But talking in a way my brother never talked.

"Also near the house there was a huge oak, full of squirrels, owls, weasels, and little lizards. And there were my two skinny aunts, who always used to say to me, 'How can you laugh, young lady?' when I was laughing. Afterward they'd go off, stiff and shriveled, through the fields. We never knew what they intended to do there, except maybe to talk with the Lord, whom one of them called 'Tom' in a familiar way, for reasons we never knew. 'It might be time now to teach these children about the love of Tom.' 'Love' affected us deeply, my sister and me. She used to giggle under her sheets.

We never went to sleep right away after we heard that word. And we never spoke it, either. Between ourselves, we took to calling love 'Tom,' too. When you come down to it, of course we were following in the true tradition: 'Love' and 'God' were the same word.

"Bitter, and delighted, I witnessed my sister's happiness. She got married. The household was breaking up. I knew it was going to be rebuilt, but in different surroundings. And, I could tell, for different purposes too. I felt that, up until then, we'd inhabited my father's happiness, not our own. The tall oak, the distant fields, my mother, my aunts, the big, easygoing horses: These were what my father had surrounded himself with from the beginning. We'd come along afterward, we children. We'd made the most of what was there. My father's silence had become the silence of the Whites. His happiness had become ours. Now we had to build our own happiness, when his kept suiting us so well. It's even more strangely complicated than that. Yes, I still had the same joys: The big oak still held its birds, the little weasels still had their burrows between its roots. Every morning, my father set out on his heavy horse, hardly more slowly than before. But when my aunt talked about 'Tom,' it was my sister's and my 'Tom' that I thought about.

"It felt very bitter to find myself walking alone. And I envied her marriage. I'm going to say something shocking. But the truth often lies in shocking things. I wanted to find happiness for myself. But if a fire from heaven had descended and killed everybody around me in the house, except for one of my brothers . . . then, in that place I loved, with the virtues I longed for the most right next to me, then I would truly have found my happiness. And this dream wasn't monstrous or perverse, it was simply natural. I was a nineteen-year-old girl, on her own since her sister had married. Around me was my father's house, full of a contentment that I loved. Now, I know I was a fool, more than anything. Silly and naïve. Aside from my family, I'd never really had heartfelt relations, except with the night, which covered my bedroom window with stars.

"Of course, I married one of my older brother's friends. Good men are disconcerting. You never know what rules their affections. Sometimes the reasons run counter to nature. Harold brought this man to visit us many times. Eventually I came to feel he was similar to my brother. Not in appearance, but he had my brother's manner. One day I caught him watching, and then imitating, a gesture Harold used to make: taking his cigar case out, opening it, half closing it, and blowing across the top of it. Certain movements of his shoulders as well. In the evening, Harold would sit down in an armchair, stretch out his legs, set his elbow on the back of the chair, and, a moment later, rest his forehead in his hand. One evening, Danny sat down, stretched his legs out, set his elbow on the back of the chair, and after exactly the same, brief moment, rested his forehead in his hand. I don't know if that wasn't what made me love him. How is one supposed to be wise to all the tricks?

"No, now...you...don't talk. And let's go back."

———

The next day, toward four o'clock in the afternoon, Adelina and Herman were standing on the expanse of heath that overlooks the Severn estuary. The land—utterly empty, uninhabited, wavelike, covered in heather—stretched out of sight in every direction, except to the west, where the blue-green foliage of the Bristol Canal was shimmering. A fanfare of horns and trumpets burst out, abruptly, to their right.

"Those are the fox hunters," said Adelina. "I have to wait until they've gone."

They heard the galloping of the horses, the cries, even the jingling of the bits.

"But you won't see them," said Adelina. "They'll pass by like shadows. What look to us like little ripples, from here, are actually slopes that drop into deep valleys and intersect each other. This huge plain looks flat, but it's really crisscrossed with secret movements. My carts should be coming from over there, where evening's turning the heather dark."

They'd arrived here hand in hand. First, they'd encountered a solitary man, planted upright as a tree, who looked like he was waiting. He greeted them, then turned on his heels.

"Give me your hand," Adelina said. "Soon we're going to have to part." After that, they walked in silence.

"The sound of those horns and trumpets," said Herman, "moved me deeply, I don't know why."

"They were playing the opening bars of a Handel concerto."

"I've never listened to much music," he said.

"You have heard," she said, "the wind and the sea. Anyone who's listened to the sounds of the elements has listened to music. Pitt knows how to play the harmonium. One evening, when he was playing some music by that very same Handel (a chorus from *Theodora*—'Venus laughing from the skies'), my father said (sometimes he spoke to the farmhands who would spend the evening with us)...he called out to Bill, who was listening too, 'I'm thinking,' my father said to him, 'about the field that runs down the hillside near the Worsleys'.

We'll have to sow it during a westerly if we don't want the wind to make away with our seed.' And Bill answered, 'I was thinking exactly the same thing, sir.'"

"And so that music had drawn the two of them to the very same place," Herman said.

"Yes, while I myself was being drawn to other places."

"I really do understand. Just like Handel, no doubt, had something other than the Worsleys' hillside in mind when he was writing his music. Is that what you meant?"

"Exactly," she said. "Listen, a minute ago it must have been a big, stout squire who blew on his horn. 'I'll be damned,' he might have said, 'if I have in mind to do anything but make a racket when I'm blowing on it.' But he probably plays the horn in a philharmonic in Berkeley, or somewhere nearby, and that brilliant ensemble must have played the Handel concerto recently. When he wanted to make a racket for the foxhunt, up on his big draft mare, the melody came back to him. (Maybe it had something to do, as well, with these endless stretches of heather in bloom.) And the other hunters fell into unison, with their horns and trumpets, and Handel came and touched you. The fox must be scared out of its wits."

"I don't know what shape the fox is in," said Herman, "or what Handel was thinking about when he set those horns playing along with those trumpets, but they suddenly spoke to me as if I'd been destined to hear them, and I'd been waiting for them all my life."

"It's the same for me," she said. "I'm just an insignificant carter of wheat. I beg you, don't pay any attention to me. What I say is of no importance. But right now I'm full of grandiose ideas with no logical connection, unless they're akin to these unfenced heaths we've been walking through. I've never been able to stand still in the middle of such expanses—they stretch away with so much power—without immediately allowing myself the freedom to ponder my most cherished dreams. Thank you for holding my hand. (You see, I don't know what I'm saying.) And thank you for walking along beside me and not talking about the one thing you'd really like to say."

"The fact is," he said, "that I'm pathetically trying to gain some time. But you're wrong to say you're nothing but an insignificant carter of wheat. It's extremely important to transport wheat. The people who wait for it must agree. Give us our daily bread."

"But give us our daily mountain town too, and Handel's horns. Give us each day our wide-open spaces. For instance, you—you're a poet—"

"I'd rather we didn't talk about that," he said. "Look, let's talk about Pitt instead, if you don't mind. Sorry for calling him by that familiar name."

"You couldn't make me happier. But don't worry. I say you're a poet like I'd say you have blond or brown hair. It's a simple observation, as though I were calling you a Lloyd's insurance agent."

"I accept the Lloyd's insurance agent label."

"When you're used to living in unbounded spaces, on land or at sea, you're naturally inclined to come up with grandiose solutions to the problems life poses. Take sailors, for example. But imagine people who live incessantly inside four walls, surrounded by towns that become more and more crowded, towns that are drenched in rain.

"Here, of course, you get swept away by the big line of the horizon—right there in front of us. It comes out of the haze, over there, and runs over there, where it plunges into the sea mists. Look how it glides across, like it possesses a kind of confidence, a certainty it will exist forever. How could we possibly ignore it? And, as long as we have to make use of our minds, how could we possibly stop them from acting the same way? But if you're boxed in, with the rugs and the fireplace, and the four servants, and the secretaire, and the library, and the files, and the index cards....

"Listen, last winter my husband made me hold a reception. He has political ambitions. If the men who were there—and believe me, they were sitting up and panting like dogs around me—if they had known they were dealing with nothing but a common smuggler (even if the only thing they'd known was that I come here, to this isolated heath, to keep an ear out for the sound of the carts, and that afterward I get on the ferry with some sacks of wheat), I believe they'd all have been shocked and dismayed, as if they couldn't imagine me capable of such vulgarity. They all have very well-defined ideas about how to govern. John Russell himself is like a babe in arms next to them. Even so, because I have a reputation for being a bit wild (and even more so, because they have to shine in front of us ladies in our bare-shouldered gowns), they got to talking about poetry, about... poems, about the poetry of life, just chitchat really! Oh, if only you'd seen their lips! And their monocles. How they let them drop off, how they put them back on with their chins held high, how they suddenly bent their heads toward me: 'Is that not so, dear friend?...' All of them a bit roguish. And, because of that, clever. And in the end, they were outdone by their subject, the poet, a little fellow convinced that his personal aims controlled human destiny, who said, 'Woe be to him who stands in the way of destiny.'"

"He was right," Herman replied, his voice animated. "And it amounts to a self-evident truth. To be opposed to destiny is a misfortune in itself. But I'd hardly give two pennies for my life if I didn't suffer from that particular misfortune."

"You have to understand," she said, "what he meant was purely personal. What it meant—and believe me, nobody, myself included, misunderstood—was: 'I'll bring woe to the poet who won't comply with the destiny I'm charting for humanity, who won't share my view.' You understand? On one who won't serve me. And yes, there you have it. Oh my, don't I entertain important people! And, to a certain extent, that little fellow was entitled to turn it into a personal affair."

"No," said Herman. "Woe to the poet, yes! (God forbid I should be one.) But your little fellow has nothing to do with it. Don't you see, Adelina? To be a poet is to stay a step ahead of human destiny. The poet doesn't follow; he isn't against anything; he's a step ahead. And he doesn't serve. To be obliged to live this way is reason enough for unhappiness."

Evening was coming on. They heard the sound of carts and a whip cracking.

"Another minute," he said. "Look." He nodded at the grass pressed flat behind them. "Isn't that the imprint of someone huge who just came to land behind us?"

"Yes," she said, "it certainly is. And you could say the imprint was made while you were talking."

"Well, look up there now!"

Awe-inspiring clouds had spread wide, like the wings of a gliding bird.

"What is it?" she asked.

He lowered his voice: "An angel."

"Whose?"

"Mine."

"Guardian?" she asked.

"Yes. Prison guard." He made a wrestling motion.

"Is it beating you?"

"Oh, no," he said, "this is something entirely different: We're beating each other."

"Farewell," she said.

In his hand, he still held the warmth of hers. In the meantime, night had fallen; the only gleam that lingered lay above the sea; and far away, at right angles to the channel, the ferryboat had already reached open water.

———

Back in the United States, he declares, "I don't have a moment to lose. I have a long-held dream. I was biding my time. Now I'm going to fulfill it." He's going to settle down in the Berkshires. He buys an old farm named Arrowhead. Surrounding the house, vast stretches of grassland rise and fall, undulate and flow toward a dizzying mass of elm and birch leaves. And, beyond the trees, the hills heave the earth and press it down.

He gets his house in order, rebuilds the chimney, paints the façade, secures the ivy, props up the weathervane, oils the hinges, adds new windows. "Herman," Mistress Melville says to him, "your head is embalmed."

It's a wonderful region. Phenomenal flocks of birds are constantly whipping up the foliage. Everything's singing, everything's flowering all of the time. In the still of the night, once the nightingale has quieted down, you hear the wild does bleating, softly, as they graze on the arbor's Virginia creeper.

"Yes," he says, "you see, it was something I wanted and needed to accomplish quickly. There are certain urges I have to get rid of this way."

He doesn't go into details, but you can plainly see that

he's launching himself headfirst into a multitude of dreams; that in the twinkling of an eye he's stood them on their feet and spanked them, like newborns, and brought them to life. But not long afterward, he abandons them. Some evenings, if you hadn't told him it had been a beautiful day, that it was a lovely evening and was going to be a wonderful night, he wouldn't have been any the wiser.

He's neighbors with his friend Nathaniel Hawthorne, whom he admires with a passion. They stroll along the country lanes or through the fields together.

"You see," Herman says to him, "this situation can't last. I'm in the grip of strange, conflicting desires. Everything's all right, of course—everybody faces the same lot in life—but, you see, you never know exactly what you have in your heart. It's quite possible that what's there, in my case, might be a bit hypocritical toward my own self. I'm going to get working. Just lately, in connection with certain thoughts, I've remembered a strange story about a whale.

"Around 1810, this whale was to the lee of the island of Mocha, off the coast of Chile. They attacked it more than a hundred times, and more than a hundred times the whale was the victor. You could even say the whale put to flight (that's the very term for it), that it put to flight three English whaling ships by leaping at them while they were beating a retreat. When it leapt at them, it really did come clear out of the sea, right up to the level of the guardrails. This whale quickly became famous. You couldn't round Cape Horn without wanting to have a go at it. Because of its age, or maybe because of some freak of nature, it was as white as snow. When you saw it from a distance, you could never tell if it was the whale, or a cloud lying low at the horizon. And every time you encountered another ship on the open sea,

you'd shout out, 'Say, do you have any news of Mocha-Dick?'
And so, I remembered all of that, I don't know why. This
unattainable thing...do you understand?"

A few months later, he'll tell Hawthorne, "Yes, I'm working." He must have written the same to Adelina, and it must
have been in the flush of embarking on a project. He was
intoxicated with the new story. She received an epic sort of
letter and wrote back, "In my eyes, with your superhuman
strength, you're the very image of struggle and victory."

Later on, she'll say to him, "I now have such a keen sense
of you that, even from afar, I can guess from your letters—
their rhythm, their composition, your handwriting—whether
you're in the throes of your work or taking a little break."
The breaks are hikes, which he now takes on his own, at full
tilt across the hills, his pockets stuffed with paper and pen-
cils, seeing nothing around him but the sea, the sea, the sea,
and then, at the bottom of the valley, his house, which looms
out, and toward which he quickly bends his course, so as to
return and write.

"This unattainable thing, do you understand," he says one
day to Hawthorne, "this unattainable thing that stands in
the way of my life."

"What is it, then, that you want to talk about?" asks
Hawthorne.

"Is there anything I've said I want to talk about, other
than that white whale?"

"Of course not," says Hawthorne. "But each time, there's
an inward-sounding tone to your words. You seem to be
wrapped up in a private passion."

"No," says Herman, after a moment. "Let's put it the other
way around: I'm wrapped up in a kind of general passion.
Should we have anything to fight against," he says, smiling,

"but the gods who oppose us? Well, what do you think, Hawthorne? Isn't it true? Imagine somebody who eventually takes up the sword, or the harpoon, to start a fight against God himself."

"It's better not to believe."

"In whom?"

"In God."

"On the contrary. Because then, where would the value be?"

"Or the madness."

"Or the madness, if you like. No, I'm thinking, on the contrary, about someone who could see God as clearly as he sees his own nose in the middle of his own face, so to speak, as clearly as the white whale up above the waters. Someone who, seeing the whale in all its glory, and being at the same time acquainted with all of its mystery, and knowing to what lengths it can go in the frenzy of its power (but never, ever forgetting the wounds with which this God has disfigured him), would, even so, hurl himself toward him and launch the harpoon."

"I think you're writing a beautiful book," says Hawthorne, after a pause.

It's *Moby-Dick*, which was finished at the beginning of 1851 and appeared the same year. *Dublin University Magazine* said, "This is an incomparable book." William P. Trent, in *A History of American Literature*, said, "This is Melville's masterpiece. Never have we had, in this way, in a book, the breathing of the seas, the passion of the winds, the suction of the depths. The most indifferent reader ends up being drawn into the demoniacal pursuit of Captain Ahab, and the invincible whale is one of the most wonderful creations of a great poet." John Masefield said, "Here are to be found the secrets of the sea. This book stands alone among all the books I know. Nothing else comes close to it." *Harper's New Monthly Magazine* of December 1851 said, in the course of an article that was ten pages long, "It is written in letters of blood....You feel the grandeur of the oceans...the magnificent savagery of a Macbeth of the seas...lifted up by his poetic genius, like the winds of the main." John Freeman said, "This is a creation as pure as *Paradise Lost*."

"So what's the matter with you, my dear," Hawthorne says to him. "For at least a month you've been looking worried. And let's come right out with it: unhappy. You definitely have the look of an unhappy man. Day by day I've been hoping to see you regain your good spirits, but I see instead that your anxiety gets darker and darker. Is it really so bad? What is it about? Can't I be of any help to you? The reviews are wonderful. Did you see Salt's last article in *The Gentleman's Magazine*? And your book is a masterpiece, beyond a doubt. You should talk to me, you know. It will surely comfort you."

"Yes, I'm uneasy," says Herman. "We're almost in February and...I'm waiting for news from a friend in England. He's never gone for more than a month without writing me. Soon it will be four months since I've received anything from him."

The last letter he'd received from her was dated October 1851. "I'm sick," she wrote. "I look charming in my bed, if you can imagine that. I sneeze, I cough, I smell of camphorated alcohol and mandarins. That's why my letter is so short and confused. Bah! I'm sending it anyway!"

"I wonder if she's read it," he says one day, in an undertone.

"What do you mean?" Hawthorne asks.

"I was just in the midst of wondering," says Herman, "if that friend of mine has read my book."

"Oh, you know," says Hawthorne, "with the publicity in

Harper's, and how quickly the name of a masterpiece spreads far and wide, your *Moby-Dick* must be as famous as *The Times*. It's impossible that your friend wouldn't have read it."

"Yes," says Herman. "And all the more so, because then I'd be really cursed. . . ."

"What are you thinking about?" asks Hawthorne.

"I'm thinking," says Herman, "what if that person died just before the book appeared?"

A year later, he's just about ended all his strolls with Hawthorne. He rarely goes out. Now and then he encounters his friend at the end of the hedgerow.

"Are you working, at least?" asks Hawthorne.

"Yes. But only because I have to."

"Have you had any news from your friend in England?"

"No, never again."

The book he's working on is called *Pierre*. When it appears, Hawthorne feels very embarrassed to talk to his friend about it. In the end, Hawthorne says, "It's a book."

"No," says Herman.

"Oh, I've tried everything," he says, four years later. "You see, Hawthorne, I've just written *Israel Potter*, but this time, this is my last book. I won't write any more. This one's a bit better than *Pierre*, but it's all I'm capable of now. Every time, I have to push myself, to force myself. It takes whiplashes. Oh! Obviously, if you look at it as a triumph of the will over revulsion, then that's what it is, and by that token, it's still worthwhile. But as a book, as a creation, no, it has no life.

After *Moby-Dick* I was disgusted. That book I threw myself into completely, in one great go . . . well, it came too late."

"How can you say that?" says Hawthorne. "A masterpiece never comes too late; there are always people who are born after it."

"Yes, but, don't you see?" says Herman. "I'm talking selfishly, for me alone. It was utterly essential that one person not die before the book appeared."

Shortly afterward, he sells Arrowhead, leaves the Berkshires, and goes to live in New York. Then we find out that he's applied for a position as a customs inspector. It's now around the year 1857.

———

He died after thirty-four years of total silence. On the morning of September 28, 1891, when the nurse who looks after him in the daytime arrives, the night nurse says to her, "Don't take your shoes off, Mrs. Fourque, he died some hours ago."

"So that's that, then, Mrs. Andirons," she says. "It just so happens I have another old gentleman who'll probably pass away this morning too. I'd best be hurrying along, lest I be late for both of them."

"Have a bite to eat, Mrs. Fourque. I've washed him, and the carpenter has been advised. Come now, we have a few minutes of peace."

"How did he make out, then?"

"Around six o'clock, I could tell it was coming. He was talking to himself. I asked him to explain: 'What are you saying?' He was asking whether we'd received anything from England. I said, 'No, Mr. Melville, no, we haven't received anything, don't fret, sleep peacefully.'"

TRANSLATOR'S ACKNOWLEDGMENTS

It was Edmund White who first urged me to read *Pour saluer Melville*, a book he described as "mad, completely mad" (in the best sense of the word!). Now Edmund has graced the present volume with his introduction. Edwin Frank commissioned me, with generous enthusiasm, to undertake the translation. Susan Barba has proven, once again, to be a most sensitive and sure-handed editor.

Isabelle Génin, of the Université Sorbonne Nouvelle, gave me invaluable support from start to finish. She carefully annotated my drafts, helping me to navigate the shifting currents in Giono's language and thought. Along the way, she saved me from more than a handful of egregious errors. On numerous occasions, I posed thorny puzzles to Jacques Le Gall, a consummate Giono scholar. Jacques always gave me helpful advice, even when the passage in question defied definitive interpretation. As president of the Association des Amis de Jean Giono, Jacques Mény continued his unflagging efforts to promote awareness of Giono in the English-speaking world.

In Canada and the U.S., many friends have read and commented on my drafts. I owe each of them a debt of gratitude: Wendell Block, David Friend, Jennifer Levine, Baṇuta Rubess, Catherine Bush, David Wallace, Roo Borson, and Joyce Zonana.

As he did for *Hill*, my friend Claude Boutterin has created a marvelous, magical image for the frontispiece.

To my closest reader, Debbie Honickman, I dedicate this labor of love.

—P. E.

OTHER NEW YORK REVIEW CLASSICS

For a complete list of titles, visit www.nyrb.com or write to:
Catalog Requests, NYRB, 435 Hudson Street, New York, NY 10014

J.R. ACKERLEY My Dog Tulip*
RENATA ADLER Speedboat*
AESCHYLUS Prometheus Bound; translated by Joel Agee*
LEOPOLDO ALAS His Only Son *with* Doña Berta*
KINGSLEY AMIS Dear Illusion: Collected Stories*
KINGSLEY AMIS Lucky Jim*
ROBERTO ARLT The Seven Madmen*
U.R. ANANTHAMURTHY Samskara: A Rite for a Dead Man*
EVE BABITZ Slow Days, Fast Company: The World, the Flesh, and L.A.*
DOROTHY BAKER Cassandra at the Wedding*
J.A. BAKER The Peregrine
HONORÉ DE BALZAC The Human Comedy: Selected Stories*
SYBILLE BEDFORD A Favorite of the Gods *and* A Compass Error*
SYBILLE BEDFORD A Legacy*
FRANS G. BENGTSSON The Long Ships*
ALEXANDER BERKMAN Prison Memoirs of an Anarchist
GEORGES BERNANOS Mouchette
BRUCE DUFFY The World As I Found It*
DAPHNE DU MAURIER Don't Look Now: Stories
ELAINE DUNDY The Dud Avocado*
MARCELLUS EMANTS A Posthumous Confession
EURIPIDES Grief Lessons: Four Plays; translated by Anne Carson
J.G. FARRELL Troubles*
FÉLIX FÉNÉON Novels in Three Lines*
BENJAMIN FONDANE Existential Monday: Philosophical Essays*
MARC FUMAROLI When the World Spoke French
MAVIS GALLANT The Cost of Living: Early and Uncollected Stories*
MAVIS GALLANT Paris Stories*
LEONARD GARDNER Fat City*
WILLIAM H. GASS In the Heart of the Heart of the Country: And Other Stories*
THÉOPHILE GAUTIER My Fantoms
GE FEI The Invisibility Cloak
JEAN GENET Prisoner of Love
ÉLISABETH GILLE The Mirador: Dreamed Memories of Irène Némirovsky by Her Daughter*
NATALIA GINZBURG Family Lexicon*
JEAN GIONO Hill*
JOHN GLASSCO Memoirs of Montparnasse*
EDMOND AND JULES DE GONCOURT Pages from the Goncourt Journals
ALICE GOODMAN History Is Our Mother: Three Libretti*
HENRY GREEN Caught*
HENRY GREEN Living*
VASILY GROSSMAN Everything Flows*
VASILY GROSSMAN Life and Fate*
PETER HANDKE Slow Homecoming
THORKILD HANSEN Arabia Felix: The Danish Expedition of 1761–1767*
ELIZABETH HARDWICK Sleepless Nights*
ALFRED HAYES My Face for the World to See*

* Also available as an electronic book.

PAUL HAZARD The Crisis of the European Mind: 1680–1715*

ALICE HERDAN-ZUCKMAYER The Farm in the Green Mountains*

YOEL HOFFMANN The Sound of the One Hand: 281 Zen Koans with Answers*

HUGO VON HOFMANNSTHAL The Lord Chandos Letter*

BOHUMIL HRABAL The Little Town Where Time Stood Still*

DOROTHY B. HUGHES In a Lonely Place*

RICHARD HUGHES A High Wind in Jamaica*

MAUDE HUTCHINS Victorine

HENRY JAMES The New York Stories of Henry James*

TOVE JANSSON The Summer Book*

JOSEPH JOUBERT The Notebooks of Joseph Joubert; translated by Paul Auster

FRIGYES KARINTHY A Journey Round My Skull

ERICH KÄSTNER Going to the Dogs: The Story of a Moralist*

GYULA KRÚDY The Adventures of Sindbad*

SIGIZMUND KRZHIZHANOVSKY The Return of Munchausen

PATRICK LEIGH FERMOR A Time to Keep Silence*

SIMON LEYS The Death of Napoleon*

SIMON LEYS The Hall of Uselessness: Collected Essays*

H.P. LOVECRAFT AND OTHERS Shadows of Carcosa: Tales of Cosmic Horror*

DWIGHT MACDONALD Masscult and Midcult: Essays Against the American Grain*

CURZIO MALAPARTE Kaputt

JANET MALCOLM In the Freud Archives

JEAN-PATRICK MANCHETTE Fatale*

JEAN-PATRICK MANCHETTE The Mad and the Bad*

GUY DE MAUPASSANT Afloat

GUY DE MAUPASSANT Like Death*

HENRI MICHAUX Miserable Miracle

JESSICA MITFORD Hons and Rebels

NANCY MITFORD Voltaire in Love*

MICHEL DE MONTAIGNE Shakespeare's Montaigne; translated by John Florio*

HENRY DE MONTHERLANT Chaos and Night

ALBERTO MORAVIA Agostino*

JAN MORRIS Conundrum*

ÁLVARO MUTIS The Adventures and Misadventures of Maqroll

L.H. MYERS The Root and the Flower*

NESCIO Amsterdam Stories*

DARCY O'BRIEN A Way of Life, Like Any Other

SILVINA OCAMPO Thus Were Their Faces*

IRIS OWENS After Claude*

BORISLAV PEKIĆ Houses*

ELEANOR PERÉNYI More Was Lost: A Memoir*

LUIGI PIRANDELLO The Late Mattia Pascal

JOSEP PLA The Gray Noteboo

ANDREY PLATONOV Happy Moscow

ANDREY PLATONOV Soul and Other Stories

NORMAN PODHORETZ Making It*

J.F. POWERS Morte d'Urban*

QIU MIAOJIN Last Words from Montmartre*

RAYMOND QUENEAU We Always Treat Women Too Well

RAYMOND QUENEAU Witch Grass

RAYMOND RADIGUET Count d'Orgel's Ball

JULES RENARD Nature Stories*

JEAN RENOIR Renoir, My Father

TIM ROBINSON Stones of Aran: Labyrinth

LINDA ROSENKRANTZ Talk*

UMBERTO SABA Ernesto*

TAYEB SALIH Season of Migration to the North

JEAN-PAUL SARTRE We Have Only This Life to Live: Selected Essays. 1939–1975

ARTHUR SCHNITZLER Late Fame*

SIMONE SCHWARZ-BART The Bridge of Beyond*

LEONARDO SCIASCIA The Wine-Dark Sea

VICTOR SEGALEN René Leys*

ANNA SEGHERS Transit*

PHILIPE-PAUL DE SÉGUR Defeat: Napoleon's Russian Campaign

VICTOR SERGE Conquered City*

VICTOR SERGE Memoirs of a Revolutionary

VLADIMIR SOROKIN The Queue

NATSUME SŌSEKI The Gate*

DAVID STACTON The Judges of the Secret Court*

CHARLES SIMIC Dime-Store Alchemy: The Art of Joseph Cornell

RICHARD STERN Other Men's Daughters

STENDHAL The Life of Henry Brulard

ITALO SVEVO As a Man Grows Older

HARVEY SWADOS Nights in the Gardens of Brooklyn

MAGDA SZABÓ The Door*

MAGDA SZABÓ Iza's Ballad*

ANTAL SZERB Journey by Moonlight*

ELIZABETH TAYLOR A View of the Harbour*

ELIZABETH TAYLOR You'll Enjoy It When You Get There: The Stories of Elizabeth Taylor*

TEFFI Memories: From Moscow to the Black Sea*

HENRY DAVID THOREAU The Journal: 1837–1861*

ALEKSANDAR TIŠMA The Book of Blam*

LIONEL TRILLING The Liberal Imagination*

THOMAS TRYON The Other*

IVAN TURGENEV Virgin Soil

JULES VALLÈS The Child

ELIZABETH VON ARNIM The Enchanted April*

ROBERT WALSER Girlfriends, Ghosts, and Other Stories*

ROBERT WALSER Jakob von Gunten

SYLVIA TOWNSEND WARNER Lolly Willowes*

SYLVIA TOWNSEND WARNER Mr. Fortune*

SYLVIA TOWNSEND WARNER Summer Will Show*

JAKOB WASSERMANN My Marriage*

SIMONE WEIL On the Abolition of All Political Parties*

SIMONE WEIL AND RACHEL BESPALOFF War and the Iliad

GLENWAY WESCOTT The Pilgrim Hawk*

REBECCA WEST The Fountain Overflows

EDITH WHARTON The New York Stories of Edith Wharton*

T. H. WHITE The Goshawk*

JOHN WILLIAMS Augustus*

JOHN WILLIAMS Stoner*

RUDOLF AND MARGARET WITTKOWER Born Under Saturn

GEOFFREY WOLFF Black Sun*

FRANCIS WYNDHAM The Complete Fiction

JOHN WYNDHAM The Chrysalids

STEFAN ZWEIG Beware of Pity*

STEFAN ZWEIG Confusion*

STEFAN ZWEIG The Post-Office Girl*